2045

AMERICA

2045
AMERICA

Johnny D. Summers, Ph.D.

Published by Johnny D. Summers
South Prairie, Washington

* * *

Much thanks to
Dr. Donald Barker
Nathan Everett
Di Freeze
JJ McKeever
Elaine Summers
Terry Summers

Dedicated to my wife

The one for whom my world revolves and the
center of all my joy and happiness.

Contents

Foreword

IN HIS BOOK, *The Collapse of Complex Societies*, Joseph Tainter cites fiscal irresponsibility as the reason great countries eventually fail. Although greed and self-aggrandizement are the political faults that frequently drive fiscal irresponsibility, they are not the sole cause of failure. Elected leaders often pursue expensive programs in the name of progress with little concern about the country's ability to fund them. As a society matures, increased resources are required to sustain its institutions beyond the growth of new agencies. The more society spends, the less benefit it receives per dollar. To maintain their legitimacy, governments must continually mobilize their resources.

Tainter calculated the average lifespan of a democracy as 200 years. This concept is not new. In 1787, Alexander Fraser Tytler, a historian of antiquities and a professor at Edinburgh University, wrote that democracy was incapable of sustaining itself as a permanent form of government. Tytler also identified 200 years as the average lifespan of the world's great civilizations. He believed societal collapse is inevitable when voters realize they can vote themselves more benefits from public funds. Tytler theorized that any Democratic society would progress:

From bondage to spiritual faith
  From spiritual faith to great courage
    From courage to liberty
      From liberty to abundance
        From abundance to complacency
         From complacency to apathy
          From apathy to dependence
           From dependence back into bondage

The United States has survived 245 years so far. According to Dr. Tainter's timeline, the US economy will outperform most other countries but will collapse in 2040.

In 2005, when the GAO (Government Accountability Office) certified the US federal debt as nearly $8 trillion, David Walker, Comptroller General of the GAO, said that our economy needed an annual growth rate of more than 10 percent for the next 75 years to eliminate the $8 trillion national debt. By 2021, the country's debt rose to over $27 trillion, which understates the amount of debt as it does not include unfunded mandates and comprises more than 100 percent of the current GDP (Gross Domestic Product). In the booming 1990s, the US economy grew, on average, 3.2 percent annually. Therefore, 10 percent annual growth is unrealistic, and sustaining it for 75 years would be unprecedented.

In 2019, the federal government spent about one dollar for every $0.75 it received in total revenue, not including unbudgeted emergency spending. Two-thirds of the country's income went to mandatory spending on entitlements such as Social Security, Medicare, Medicaid, etc. Congress controls the other third of the nation's spending, and it appropriates about $75 billion outside of the budget as an emergency fund—which the country usually exceeds. In other words, US citizens are demanding more government than they are willing to pay for, and a reckoning is coming.

2022

WE ARE THE land of Lincoln, Roosevelt, and Reagan. They are who built America. As we progressed through Trump and Biden, many questions arose. Black Lives Matter, Antifa, white supremacy, and racism became large parts of our society's noise. Immigration continues to affect our country's electorate. These issues will be pages in our story, but will they be a large part of the American dynasty? We fought a war to end slavery. We sent millions of young Americans to fight foreign wars to profligate freedom and our way of life. We lifted millions of people out of poverty around the globe. We have given almost every

American a better quality of life than most of the world's citizens. What a great country we have… for now.

My name is Jesse Wright. On January 5, 2000, I was born in the small town of Enumclaw, Washington, where my family had lived for 15 years. Shortly after my birth, my father's employer, an aerospace company, reassigned him to its new facility in Zhoushan, China. The company needed his expertise to help expand its market for airplane sales, parts, and maintenance operations in China.

Since opportunities for Western women were scarce in China, my mother, though well-educated, spent much of her time at home. Once she had the house in order and made sure she fed me, mom avidly pursued her many interests, including reading about mid-century architecture and design, listening to American jazz, and reading historical novels. One of her interests was learning Mandarin, to which she dedicated several hours a day.

With my mother's busy schedule, no other family members around, and my father's long days at work, I relied on my toys for companionship and for learning about the world. I suppose the strong sense of self-reliance of depending on my own resources to achieve what I want was the result of those early years.

When I was three, my parents hired a local tutor to teach me Mandarin. We spoke Mandarin at home to help us adapt to our new environment. In time, I became a prolific reader and quite adept at learning new languages.

When I was ten years old, my dad's company tasked him with merging two other aerospace companies under the parent company's umbrella. For that task, my family relocated to Charleston, South Carolina.

This latest expansion was to facilitate building a new type of aircraft in a more business-friendly location. The aircraft's design involved a substantial increase in technology and efficiency. Knowing that its success would significantly impact both the company and the airline industry, my father's long hours at work were tremendously stressful.

Our house was in Goose Creek, 25 minutes north of the Charleston Airport, where my dad worked. I attended College Park Elementary School. I did well academically, but due to my early years in a different culture, I tended to feel alienated from my classmates. It took a while for me to feel like I fit in. In middle school, when I began participating in sports, I felt more comfortable socially.

My above-average athletic skills helped me become a starter on every team I committed to for all three years of middle school, and I made the honor roll every semester. By the time I got to Stratford High School, I was on friendly terms with many of my classmates. However, I never formed any close friendships and had little or no interest in socializing – mainly because I lacked both social skills and self-confidence. For some reason, a healthy confidence in my physical abilities did not extrapolate to social situations where I felt numb and inexplicably alienated from strangers. I remember realizing that it wasn't "normal," and I felt sad about it. It was easier to compartmentalize it in the back of my mind than confront the problem.

In high school, my main concern was competing with more accomplished athletes for places on the school's teams. I focused on practice, including weight and endurance training. I enjoyed the camaraderie but did not want to take time away from my studies to hang out with my teammates. The idea of dating someone was so far from a relatable experience that I could not allow myself to contemplate the reasons. By the end of my senior year, I had an excellent record with every sports team I joined and had maintained a 4.0 GPA throughout the four years.

In my senior year, to enhance my high school record, I decided to run for vice president of the student body and won. My first experience in a leadership role was surprisingly empowering; it strengthened my confidence in working successfully with other people and groups with various interests.

In 2018, I accepted a partial scholarship to the University of Texas in Austin. In the fall, I began studying computer science with a political science minor. Although I had developed a strong interest in politics from my tenure as student body vice president in high school, the job prospects seemed much better for a computer science grad than for a political science wonk.

I became interested in politics again in my junior year of college, so I ran for secretary of the junior class and won. My responsibilities included working with other class representatives to address issues important to the student body. Those concerns mirrored the outrage of most American citizens over the treatment of blacks by the police, the rise of white supremacy groups, and institutional racism and bigotry in business and government.

I was basically somewhere in the middle on most social and political issues. Still, an op-ed piece in the *Austin American-Statesman* made me realize I needed to learn the details of the problems to decide exactly where I stood, politically. The article opined those supporters of the Black Lives Matter movement who believed protesters were trying to secure the rights of historically wronged African-Americans might be funding radical organizations with Marxist leadership. Their goals were not to make the American Dream accessible to everyone but rather to transform America itself in their favor.

One group, it said, was proposing an end to all police departments and prisons and calling for a restructuring of tax codes at all governmental levels to create a sustainable redistribution of wealth among US citizens. This struck me as a bit odd. I thought about Plato's tenets of statesmanship, which I had recently read for one of my classes. The main tenet was, in effect, that public policy should be based on long-term consequences, not on immediate advantages or temporary popularity. That way, a policy would avoid risking a worse result than the issue it addressed.

University students were also protesting, including ours. Their stated interests were preventing hate speech on campus. They proposed renaming school buildings that represented oppressive historical figures and demanded removing monuments of objectionable historical figures. They also wanted an end to the spread of discriminatory ideas being propagated in some classes and removing the professors who were teaching those ideas.

Though my personal views were less controversial than those of many of my classmates, I still pursued their goals with the vigor required of my position. Once again, I thoroughly enjoyed the role of intermediary between student organizations, the school administration, and local activist groups. I worked tirelessly to build a network of contacts to help further the student body's agenda.

For the first time, I felt a sense of purpose, and I liked the feeling. My track record of success in school government bolstered my confidence. It opened my eyes to the potential impact my advocacy could have in a larger political arena, such as in the real world outside college. It tempted me to consider politics as a career path.

When I had a few extra minutes at the library, I began researching the types of jobs available in political organizations. I found vague job descriptions for research analysts, political strategy analysts, campaign analysts, and policy analysts. All of these sounded similar and mainly cerebral. Policy, it seemed to me, provided a roadmap for activism but, as words on a page, was inherently bereft of action.

College athletics not only kept me in shape, but my hours spent exercising gave me time to think through the many issues facing the country. The current events that triggered political controversy during my college years helped me formulate the fundamental values and political beliefs that I carried into adult life. For instance, the shooting at a high school in Parkland, Florida, that killed 17 people happened early in my freshman year. It prompted a week-long debate in my head about the issues around gun control. Although the Second Amendment gives all citizens the right to defend themselves, what about the safety of people who become victims of gun violence? Is the protection of a few people worth restricting the entire country's right to protect themselves with their own guns?

The former president's hard-liner immigration policies outraged many Americans, mostly Democrats and Independents, but did he go too far by separating migrant children from their parents? I wrestled with myself about the morality and compassion of this policy versus the need to take a firm stand on illegal immigration that was obviously out of control and an added burden on the country's already strained social and healthcare assistance programs.

* * *

THE WINNING CANDIDATES of the 2020 election promised economic recovery and bringing the country together. The 2022 mid-term elections took place amidst building racial tension, continued economic uncertainty, and a solid political divide.

The current administration's immigration program significantly increased the number of migrants entering the US, primarily from Central and South America. Many of them did not assimilate well and began depending on welfare and medical services, which increased the costs of those services beyond the budgeted funds of both state and federal governments.

Increases in the population of major US cities, as shown in the 2020 Census, meant an increase in urban representation in the House of Representatives. The census also revealed that Americans had fewer children than before and that deaths outnumbered births in the last decade. Immigration, therefore, accounted for the larger population of the country's growth. In addition, there was an increase in the number of elderly US citizens, which corresponded with higher federal healthcare costs in that decade.

Congress held hearings on the implications of defunding law enforcement. They addressed concerns about maintaining civil order while reducing reported injustices to underrepresented groups. The results of the Seattle Capitol Hill Occupation Protest (CHOP), an experimental, police-free "self-governing" zone, weighed heavy in their debate. Without police presence, crime increased disproportionately in a short period, which required a corresponding increase in social workers to de-escalate non-life-threatening situations. In Chicago, the CPD's Officer Support System (OSS), designed to alert supervisors when officers exhibited signs of stress or trauma, launched in the fall of 2020 with inconclusive early results. The Portland Police Bureau continued to face critical staffing shortages into 2021, reporting a deficit of 200 officers and a lack of funding to replace them. In Minneapolis, the city council voted to dismantle the police but became unsettled by the rise of crime in the following months.

The citizens then demanded immediate police action. New York City and Chicago had significant police officer reductions through early retirements and resignations, bringing their forces to the lowest level in over a decade. Many police forces were having increased difficulty recruiting new officers. Congress wanted to find answers.

Many state governors were concerned with the significant drop in tax revenue during 2020 and 2021. They attributed the deficit to the federal government's actions during the pandemic, including widespread shutdowns, reduced air travel and tourism, restaurant closures, bans on large gatherings, concerts, etc. Combined with the increased medical obligations of the Affordable Care Act, state budgets were under increasing pressure. Significantly higher unemployment claims, primarily due to layoffs from widespread closures, were up. Many states had to move people to welfare when benefits expired. These circumstances were even more concerning for states with balanced budget laws. Elected officials approached the new president and Congress for federal assistance to help alleviate the increased deficit spending that the states experienced.

Before 2020, the federal government was borrowing 25 percent of every dollar it spent. The numerous multi-trillion-dollar bailouts added significantly to the US debt. Since the debt was not a political issue at the time, the governors felt they were on a solid footing to get additional federal money to help bridge the gaps in their budgets.

An emerging economic philosophy, Modern Monetary Theory (MMT), had gathered a growing number of believers. The theory purported that federal debt was not a significant issue for countries that print their own money, such as the US, UK, China, Canada, etc. In fact, MMT claimed that deficit spending was good for the economy in most cases. The basic principle of MMT was that the federal government was the source of all funds required to finance the government, not the taxpayers. Some proponents of MMT have become advisors to Democratic and Independent legislators. Although they acknowledged that printing more money would cause inflation, raising consumer prices, and destroy investments eventually, it was a point downplayed by MMT devotees.

Increases in federal spending demonstrated that more legislators seemed to believe in MMT than in the past. When politicians think they can spend money without regard for the country's debt, they tend to find unlimited opportunities to do so.

Growing inflation was another issue the administration faced. Due mainly to disruptions in distribution, a number of products were scarce, and changes in delivery methods added higher costs to many businesses. The result was an increase in the overall cost of providing goods and services. At the end of 2022, inflation had risen to 5.7 percent, with indications it would likely continue to climb.

Public buildings, highways, and bridges, already in decline from decades of underfunding, were further damaged by demonstrations across America. Estimates for needed repairs climbed past $1 billion. In addition, many states had highways requiring repairs, and municipal buildings were in dire need of updated technology, fire suppression systems, and asbestos removal.

Before the 2020 election, the former president submitted a letter to the World Health Organization (WHO), an arm of the United Nations (UN), informing them that the US intended to withdraw its support. Although WHO had potential benefits for the country, the president had doubts about the usefulness of the UN. Many of the member nations frequently attacked US policies and voted against its agenda. The US paid over $10 billion a year to the UN, and the former president questioned the value of that contribution. Withdrawing from WHO would be the first step in his long-term goal of leaving the United Nations. However, in 2021, the new democrat president reversed that course, telling the United Nations that the US would stay and continue to fund WHO.

China had become the primary competitor to the US in several ways. As consumers, they competed as a marketplace, reducing US strength internationally by lowering demand for American products. To keep export prices low, China purchased a large volume of US treasury bonds. This curried the favor of US legislators and kept tariffs lower. China became the largest lender-nation to the US; Japan was second. Japan owned 4.7 percent of the US debt, but their percentage would decrease. Their focus was providing better economic conditions for their citizens, not building control beyond their borders. China owned eight percent, or $1.9 trillion of the US debt, comprising 15 percent of the United States' debt to foreign countries.

Although international economics had the Chinese yuan tied to the dollar, many believed the Chinese government manipulated their currency. Their goal was to replace the US dollar as the world reference currency. The dollar had been the world currency since 1944, with most international trade conducted in US dollars. Recently, China had begun using the yuan for its oil transactions with Russia. They pressured other countries to follow suit.

The US trade deficit with China was more than $283 billion by the end of 2020. US exports to China were $110 billion, and imports from China were over $393 billion. Many of the exports they received from the US were raw materials, which they used with low-cost labor to produce goods they could export. They ultimately shipped a sizeable portion of these products as imports to the US, mainly as computers, cell phones, apparel, and footwear.

Chinese President Xi Jinping defied the country's two-term limit policy and had the National People's Congress of the People's Republic of China approve him remaining leader for life. By usurping the world currency, controlling commerce, and funding US debt, China was changing world power dynamics in their favor.

At the end of 2022, the federal debt was $29.8 trillion, and debt servicing was the fastest-growing national expense. A budget to ensure another $1.5 trillion in debt was in place for 2023 without considering any natural disasters or unexpected military expenses due to our continued presence in the Middle East. This budget required an increase in the debt limit of the United States.

Due to continuing pressures from both sides of the aisle to slow the national debt, the federal government reduced the long-standing payments to states for Medicare and welfare, which required states to increase their taxes to help cover those costs. However, the reduction in federal support of social services created nearly unsurmountable pressure on many state budgets still recovering from their significant tax shortfalls during the 2020-2021 pandemic. The reduced payments made little more than a dent in the country's ever-mounting debt for the federal government.

2023

IN MY SENIOR year at the University of Texas, I campaigned hard for student body vice president and won, despite intense competition from two candidates with more experience. As second-in-command, I chaired the Assembly of College Councils and oversaw the student government training program. This valuable experience required me to learn many things quickly and think on my feet. I looked forward to every meeting and enjoyed the process of resolving problems and challenges immensely.

Midway through my senior year, I looked into my job options more closely. The IT industry was the obvious destination for computer science grads. Still, I wondered what type of tech jobs and salaries were available in the field of politics beyond doing research and programming. I wanted something more challenging that I could build on for future pursuits.

My parents, especially my father, urged me to join a major tech or aerospace company--industries that had the highest growth potential. I knew that being fluent in Mandarin would undoubtedly afford me more opportunities and a higher salary in those fields. From my previous research, I had a rough idea that jobs in political organizations, like strategists or policy analysts, started at around $75,000. The same level of position in the federal government or the CIA paid about $85,000.

I knew my parents were right. Despite feeling drawn to the world of politics, I applied to several top tech companies. Ultimately, I took a job as a global market analyst in the San Francisco office of ICBC (Industrial and Commercial Bank of China). The starting salary was $125,000, about 20 percent higher than my first salary would be without fluency in Mandarin.

After the first few months, my job required frequent trips to the company's home office in Beijing. My job involved analyzing international trade policies. I worked to advise on policies that would prevent global conflict over intellectual properties. That work also included mitigating any issues other nations voiced about China's practices.

China had been investing in foreign seaports, airports, and infrastructure entities. When countries had trouble meeting their debt servicing obligations, the Chinese government took possession of the properties, establishing a vital foothold that increased Chinese shipping opportunities and their control over other nations and companies using their ports. Needless to say, these actions created growing frictions with the countries involved.

Jittery trade tensions with the US and around the world had heightened in November of 2020 when 15 Asia-Pacific countries entered into a large and formidable free-trade pact, called the Regional Comprehensive Economic Partnership or RCEP. Member governments accounted for 30 percent of the world's GDP – more than NAFTA or the European Union. Many of the signors had also previously joined the huge free-trade pact, Trans-Pacific Partnership (TPP), which includes Canada, Mexico, Chile, and Peru.

Another task I had for my company was to look for ways to minimize conflicts and mitigate the creation of US laws regarding the ongoing, alleged unauthorized use of intellectual property by the Chinese government. Soon after China opened its markets in 2018, accusations continued of forcing US firms to transfer their technology to their Chinese business partners in exchange for access to its one billion-plus population. The Chinese government denied the accusations.

***

THE DEMOCRAT PRESIDENT pushed hard to rebuild our connection to the World Trade Organization, which had no support from Republicans. The media predominantly favored staying in the WTO. The Speaker of the House worked the back rooms to get backing from her caucus and determine which Republicans might support the president. The US did not miss any payments to stay in the WTO, paying the assessed fees of $237 million and the additional voluntary contribution of $656 million.

The size and intensity of protests to defund the police and take down monuments had diminished, but the institutional and legislative support for them strengthened. The policies sought by the protesters had become a part of some legislation with varying levels of support.

Some municipalities took steps to modify their police procedures by reducing the number of police officers and hiring social workers with special training in de-escalating conflicts.

Unfortunately, the initial result was an increase in violent crime and theft, disproportionately occurring in underprivileged areas of the cities. Some mayors attempted to rehire many of their police officers to accompany the social workers to their encounters. The move required increasing their budgets to above pre-protest levels to support the additional personnel. Recruiting was slow and expensive, and the recruits lacked the qualifications of previous generations of law enforcement officers.

The cost of ongoing wars in the Middle East was over $2 trillion annually. Neither Congress nor the president imposed spending restrictions on military action. Thus, US generals had free reign to spend, resulting in a perennial increase in the military budget without following the congressional approval process.

Interest rates had hovered artificially near historic lows over the past decade, but current economic pressures began pushing interest rates higher. That factor increased the cost of servicing future US government debt and raised the price of consumer debt and mortgages.

Few politicians discussed unfunded pension commitments. Most private companies began divesting themselves from employee retirement programs in the late 1970s because of their expense, but many municipal jobs still had defined-benefit retirements. As interest rates were lower than economic realities would suggest, companies were required to put aside more funds for retirees, which became more challenging to maintain. These obligations of funding retirement programs by private companies were not a component of public plans. Public unions for teachers, police, fire, office workers, etc., could continue their retirement programs in their contracts.

Politicians pandered to the unions to get re-elected but then later failed to fund the retirement plans adequately. Politicians could not raise taxes enough to cover the shortfall and still get re-elected. The result was nearly $7 trillion in unfunded obligations to local government retirees, representing over $20,000 per retiree household. This deficit did not show up in the federal debt. Unfunded pensions had contributed to Detroit's bankruptcy in 2013 when the auto industry's demise decimated Detroit's tax base. Through bankruptcy, Detroit nullified employee retirements, reduced medical coverage, and severely impacted those already in retirement. This sign of things to come would affect other state and municipal governments as their budgets became strained.

In the late 1800s, the French decided to build a canal through Central America. The debate was whether to construct the canal in Nicaragua, which had a large lake and less treacherous terrain, or Panama, which required a shorter canal, but because of the landscape, the engineering challenge was horrific. The French decided to build a canal without locks in Panama. The jungles were dangerous for the unprepared French. After an untold number of malaria and yellow fever deaths, the French gave up on the canal. They left millions of dollars' worth of equipment and supplies behind. At the turn of the century, the United States picked up the mantle. In 1914, the Panama Canal opened with locks to ship passage. The US maintained control of the canal until December 31, 1999, when Panama took back total control of the waterway.

The Panamanians made significant modifications to the canal in 2016, requiring billions of dollars in investment. China provided most of the funds. When the canal needed additional funding to address maintenance on the aging locks, China again provided most of the financing.

Through all revenue sources, the US government had $4.6 trillion in revenue. It was a steady growth in income for the treasury, but not enough to cover spending. The federal debt at the end of 2023 was 33.8 trillion. The budget for 2024 was to ensure another $3.38 trillion without considering any natural disasters or unexpected military charges due to our continued presence in the

Middle East. This budget twice required an increase in the debt limit of the United States.

2024

THIS YEAR WAS the first presidential campaign in which I became involved. I decided that the Republican Platform was more in line with my own beliefs. In August, the Republican party made a few changes to the 2020 Platform. They added a more substantial resolution to re-commit to invigorating private-sector institutions so they would not erode further into centralized social planning. It also stressed its commitment to restoring US military strength around the world, stating, "Tyranny and injustice thrive when America is weak."

On international policy, the GOP warned about an emboldened China. They re-affirmed a

US leadership role in our Asian Pacific alliances with Japan, South Korea, Australia, Thailand, and the Philippines. They expressed concern over China's return to Maoism. The Republicans warned about China's continued government and military threats aimed at intimidating countries in Southeast Asia, especially on the Asian Pacific rim. China's strength in enforcing these threats would be problematic for US interests.

It seemed obvious the federal government was too big and overly involved in too many aspects of our lives. I believe that if individuals worked together to solve the problems local governments faced, it would reduce the need for federal intervention. Our country could have a much smaller public workforce.

I was not a Libertarian, but I wasn't convinced that a strong centralized government was entirely a bad thing. There was an unarguable need for government to protect property rights and provide public safety for its citizens. I would stay on the fence for another year or so before I defined my stance on too much government interference in the lives of the American people.

Gun control continued as a huge national issue, especially in major metropolitan areas and college campuses. Of course, students' views at the University of Texas differed significantly from those of young people on most US campuses. Texas

Longhorn students believed strongly in their right to bear arms. The faculty, however, didn't seem to agree. The school administration stifled pro-gun rallies on campus by denying rally permits to pro-second amendment rights students. When they gathered to protest anyway, the police intervened to break up the assemblies. However, the administration did issue permits to anti-gun organizations, which pro-gun-rights students complained about to the administration to no avail. Student publications and social media sites vilified pro-second amendment students within the University.

The intensity of the 2024 presidential election was even more contentious than the attacks during the 2020 election cycle. The bar of civility remained low. Human decency had lost out to the drive for power. No insult, no lie, no disrespect was too strong as long as it was perceived to pick up one additional vote. Both political parties pointed fingers at their opponents as the culprit of deception.

The venom was worse in battleground states. In the end, the Democratic nominee won the presidency with 315 electoral votes, and liberals increased their majority in Congress. The Republicans maintained 192 seats, whereas the Democrats controlled 243 seats. The Senate remained in Democratic hands by two seats (51 to 48, with one independent who leaned Democratically.) The balance of power was unchanged.

* * *

BY 2024, THE US population had grown steadily at about 3.5 percent. That growth, however, was attributed to immigration, both legal and undocumented. There had been a drop in population growth of US citizens by 36 percent over the last ten years, an average loss of 3.6 percent per year. The ramification was that more American citizens were dying than being born. In 2024, the overall growth rate of the US population was a mere 0.2 percent.

In addition, the fertility rate was 1.62 births per child-bearing aged woman, the lowest in US history. It takes a rate of 2.1 to maintain a stable level of population. This slowing of population growth resulted in higher elder care costs as the older baby boomer generation continued to retire. The rise of the retired population required additional expenditures for social security resources and healthcare. There were fewer working people to fund these programs. The result was increased deficit spending outside of the normal budgetary process.

After several years of study and debate, the Department of Global Change (DGC) became a new presidential cabinet position. The Department of the Interior focused on US territories; the DGC worked with US industry to reduce the human impact on our environment. Their secondary mission was to work with foreign nations to reduce their carbon emissions.

Although the government could exert pressure on US companies to comply through legislation or executive order, foreign countries could not. For that purpose, DGC funding came from monetary incentives to promote their goals, making them one of the highest funded agencies at $500 billion annually. For years to come, their budget increased at a rate higher than inflation.

The new mail-in ballot voting system of 2020 was seen as a disaster by Republicans. The one-term president had filed lawsuits in many states claiming fraudulent voting and voter tampering. Although the Republicans spent the next couple of years fighting further blanket mail-in ballots, the Democrats were successful in most states and many jurisdictions to increase the technique. Liberals claimed the old system, which required in-person voting, was unfair to minorities and the less fortunate, who were often unable to make it to the polls. Democrats believed "every vote counted" and wanted to ensure every voice was heard.

By the 2024 election season, most of the state's secretaries of state had invested the resources to make the process more transparent. Although the election season was just as contentious for the politicians, the voting process was much smoother and had fewer lawsuits. As usual, the losing politician felt cheated.

The US president submitted his budget proposal for 2025 that had the government spending $2.2 trillion more than projected revenue. The funding had increases in infrastructure to help with repairs after years of neglect. Most pundits believed the increases were woefully inconsequential for the magnitude of the decay. There was additional untargeted funding for cities and states to help with welfare, retirement funding, and women's programs.

The Treasury issued $3.38 trillion in securities in 2024. The interest rate for these bonds increased to 3.5 percent, with a steady increase over four years. The increased interest made debt payments higher and raised the federal budget without an increase in government services.

China did not want the US dollar as the world's global currency and looked for ways to impose their yuan into world financial activity. To further their cause, the Chinese government untethered the yuan from the US dollar. As their economy grew, it became easier for countries to deal directly with China with the yuan, weakening the US dollar and increasing the money supply, causing higher inflation in America.

The 2024 Democratic presidential nominee promised to raise taxes only on people making over $400,000 a year. However, after the election, he acknowledged that the tax increase would not adequately pay for all his proposed programs. The compromise that caused the least pushback was to raise taxes on families making over $165,000 per year. The president also succeeded in getting a 40 percent increase on people in the upper brackets. It meant families making over $165,000 paid 33.7 percent income tax, while families in the top category, making over $600,000, paid a rate of 51.8 percent.

There was a reversal in the view of the estate tax. The protected amount went down to $5 million, and the percentage tax increased to 40 percent across the board.

It was also not helpful that other nations, like Russia, did not like US dominance and its influence over world affairs. Russia seemed happy to deal with China using the yuan. Other countries followed, and this lessened China's concern regarding the valuation of the US dollar. Central banks began holding yuan, thus increasing the demand and lowering interest rates on yuan-based bonds and reducing exporter costs.

China's share of international trade and gross domestic product grew to over 19 percent. It was the second most used currency in the world. The yuan had become a reserve currency in 2015, with China's ultimate goal of becoming the world's global currency, supplanting the US dollar.

The weakening of the US dollar helped China's yuan. In recent years, investors and bankers began questioning the transparency and accuracy of US government accounting and reporting, believing their debt was higher than reported. For the first time, America's ability to repay its debt came into question.

The federal debt at the end of 2024 was $37.2 trillion, and another $3.72 trillion deficit scheduled for 2025. Again this didn't take into account natural disasters or military emergencies, and the US had to increase the debt limit yet again.

2025

SINCE MY HIRING two years ago, the focus of my work had shifted from analyzing trade policies to helping to mitigate an increasing number of intellectual property theft lawsuits filed against Chinese companies by the US and other countries. It required frequent trips to Washington, D.C., as well as to major European cities, in addition to being at my home office in Beijing.

China's "Thousand Talents Program" was one of more than 200 other recruitment plans that targeted the US and other foreign academics and researchers to work in China. Chinese officials openly described their goal as a way to access critical intellectual properties for their own programs and pursuits. The US described it as a blatant scheme to steal US technology and trade secrets, contributing to the unrest between the countries. However, the massive trade between the countries made a strong response from the US unpalatable as it would negatively affect our economy.

The US response was to set up a Commission on Theft of American Intellectual Property. It estimated the annual cost to our country in the range of $225 to $600 billion in 2018. By 2020, the US Justice Department had begun taking more decisive action to clamp down on Chinese economic espionage. The department sentenced a professor at Emory University to one year of probation for his connection to the Thousand Talents Program, which he had hidden from the federal government. A former engineering professor at an Atlanta-based university faced arrest for failing to disclose his ties to Chinese businesses and China's government. The commission had its successes, but the financial impact on the US economy continued.

When the US Justice Department launched an investigation into three researchers hiding their work for the Chinese government, my company sent me to Washington, DC, to learn as much about the investigation as possible. My supervisor supplied me with a list of contacts, including some Democratic and Republican committee members.

I found my first direct foray into Washington's bureaucracy quite exciting, and I felt comfortable in the bustling atmosphere of methodical, agenda-focused officialdom. After a year of intense focus on this assignment, my company began to reduce the number of lawsuits filed against them and even had a few cases dropped.

During one of my home-office stays in Beijing, I befriended a pleasant young woman who worked in the international trade department of my company. She had relocated from Shanghai. One afternoon we met her boyfriend from Shanghai at a Starbucks Café in Beijing, and after that, the three of us became close friends. They were my first real friends in China. When I spent time with them, I felt more relaxed and accepted than I ever had before.

Surprisingly, my company showed appreciation for my work on their behalf by sending me to a one-year Executive Masters in Business Administration program at Stanford University.

***

STUDENT LOAN DEBT had been a festering political issue for the last ten years. During the 2024 presidential campaign, it surfaced again when American students owed nearly $2 trillion in education loans. It represented almost twice the budget for the Department of Defense and over 20 times the Department of Education's funding. Although only 14 percent of Americans had student loans, a large percentage of citizens had children who could potentially be attending college. Therefore, more than 60 percent of Americans supported free college tuition. As with other subsidized programs, costs would probably outpace inflation and government projections. The estimated cost of making public universities free was $88 billion per year; based on historical precedence if implemented the actual price proved to be much higher.

As the federal deficit exceeded $3.7 trillion, there was pressure to increase revenue. Although significant tax increases on high-income earners and corporations were politically palpable, the Government Accountability Office numbers indicated these changes would not generate enough revenue to make a meaningful difference in the deficit or the ongoing debt. A broader tax increase was needed, which was problematic for the president and Congress. Although they had just taken office, the backlash was a tender issue. The result was a two percent increase in all tax brackets. It was a compromise that only moderately offended voters and partially covered the shortfall—in theory. The resulting tax revenue was considerably less than projected. Based on the rosy projections, Congress increased spending.

The Social Security trust fund was severely underfunded. The federal government increased the withholdings by just over ten percent, from 6.2 percent to 7.2 percent. The income that was subject to the tax was increased eleven percent from $137,700 to $154,000. These were the projected changes that would keep the fund solvent for an additional twenty years.

The nationwide legalization of marijuana began to reduce the costs of America's drug war. Yet, the Drug Enforcement Administration (DEA) budget remained high. Their expenditures were four times their capital receipts, costing the federal government $2.5 billion annually. The DEA budget continued to increase due to political maneuvering by experienced bureaucrats in the administration.

On October 31, 2025, a 7.3 magnitude earthquake occurred, centered just offshore in Huntington Beach, California. The Halloween earthquake caused over $17 billion in damage to Los Angeles alone, with Orange County sustaining an additional $15.4 billion. The total death toll was nearly 800.

The federal government responded with emergency services to provide food, water, and medical services. The Navy's *USS Mercy* was moved from San Diego, its homeport, to Los Angeles to help with casualties. In the end, the federal government spent $9 billion in immediate response, then $25 billion in rebuilding assistance. Because the state and local governments had no budget for disaster relief, the remainder of the repairs were paid for by a bond issuance for $9 billion that foreign investors primarily funded.

China strengthened its hold on the pharmaceutical industry. Over 65 percent of medicines distributed in the US came from China in the early 2020s, making them cheaper for pharmacies and US insurance companies. It was another political problem for US pharmaceutical companies and Congress. In a given year, companies spent billions researching new drugs, of which only one might become marketable. Citizens complained that a pill cost $100 when it only cost the pharmaceutical company $0.25 to make. The problem was that it cost $0.25 to make the second pill. The first one cost $25 billion due to research expenditures. When China knocked off pharmaceutical companies' technology, it disincentivized innovation and investment in research, thus delaying getting life-saving medicines to market.

The US government had revenue of $4.83 trillion in 2026. The federal debt at the end of 2025 was $40.9 trillion, and another $4.09 trillion deficit budgeted for 2026, without any contingencies for emergency funding and a standing military presence in the Middle East. Another debt limit increase passed Congress for the United States.

2026

AFTER GRADUATING FROM Stanford's Executive Masters in Business Administration program, I went to my company's Dallas office as a computer technology sharing department manager. Many of my duties were the same, but networking with power brokers was a new key responsibility.

In 2020, the US Commission on Theft of American Intellectual Property estimated that the cost to American companies was between $315 to $710 billion annually. It implied that a large portion of the cost was attributable to Chinese businesses. Although the US had intensified its efforts to curb the losses in the years since the start of the commission, customs and border patrol officials reported that 87 percent of counterfeit goods they seized annually originated in China.

Initially, China started a program of cloning US business operations. Companies had set up factories in China to take advantage of low manufacturing costs. For example, when a motorcycle company built a factory in China, a year later, a new Chinese factory opened that started making the same motorcycles with a similar logo to the US companies. They could sell the motorcycles much cheaper because they didn't spend money on product design and development. The Boeing Company, a manufacturer of airplanes, rotorcraft, rockets, satellites, telecommunications equipment, and missiles, also transferred technology unwittingly to China.

In Boeing aircraft, the wing design is the secret ingredient that makes them competitive. The wing contains a complicated array of flight control systems, fuel systems, landing gear, engine mounts, etc. When Boeing wanted to establish a factory in China to build non-wing parts for their planes, the Chinese government convinced them that it would be a better deal for Boeing if they constructed the enigmatic wing in their country.

Shortly after the Boeing factory in China began producing Boeing wings, COMAC, Commercial Aircraft Corporation of China, opened. The increased competition cost Boeing billions of dollars in sales and tens of thousands of high-paying jobs in the US.

Based on Gross Domestic Product (GDP), at the end of 2026, China passed the US as the world's largest economy. With a $24.34 trillion economy, China renewed its efforts to make its yuan the primary international currency. The US government fought this change. If the yuan became the global currency, there would be a flood of US dollars as countries transitioned their reserves of hard currency. The result would be a significant increase in US inflation.

Those intrusions into American ingenuity are old problems. Since the 1980s, China has worked in the telecommunications and internet industries. Their goal was to steal intellectual properties (IP) that allowed them to manufacture cell phones, notebooks, and computer systems, giving them access to an individual's personal information. A Chinese corporation was like a Trojan horse for their tech companies. At first, it seemed innocuous that they would know who their customer's friends were; but it gave them access to financial data, medical records, and search and spending habits. It was all meant to target their customers for commerce, but it also made individuals and corporations susceptible to hacking and exploitation.

In 2020, the US national security adviser warned that China's goal was to use the US to supply raw materials, agricultural products, and energy to fuel the Chinese production of industrial and consumer goods. According to the security advisor, China's goal was a "modern-day version of the tributary system" with an imperial China at its center. Few things aided this agenda more directly than the Chinese theft of US intellectual property. According to the Federal Bureau of Investigation (FBI) director, China's intellectual property theft represented the most significant transfer of wealth in history. It accounted for the degradation in the quality of life for millions of Americans, requiring them to take lesser jobs, if they could even find a job.

* * *

AFTER YEARS OF promising free state college education for Americans, the federal government enacted it into law. Families with a household income of less than $140,000 for single earners or $200,000 for dual earners were eligible for their kids to receive free tuition, books, and fees at state universities. Students with outstanding loans had them forgiven. The cost of the loan forgiveness was $1.78 trillion. Government funding of state university attendance was $103 billion the first year and climbed each year exponentially.

Spending increased on renewable energy. In 2018, the cost per megawatt was approximately $75. That cost plunged and averaged between $3 to $7 per megawatt. The government subsidized green energy with three trillion dollars the previous five years. To broaden the usage of renewable energy, the federal government added two trillion dollars in subsidies in 2026. That figure increased five percent a year into perpetuity. There were still many obstacles to green energy. Because energy becomes lost in transmission, the solar panels and wind turbines needed to be near the power consumers. However, citizens did not like having those sources in their backyard. Old-world energy resources were still a component in providing green energy. Oil produced most of the electricity needed to charge electric cars. It would take more time and money to close the chasm.

At 86 years old, the Speaker of the House died. Great fanfare marked the state funeral. Her family had her body laid to rest in San Francisco, in the district she represented for five decades. The new Democratic speaker was 52 years old, and in an interview, articulated her hope to also stay in the job for decades. She also expressed great hope for the current direction of the progressive agenda and put forth several new programs to benefit the less fortunate people of our country.

The Chinese government methodically increased military spending as they expanded their global presence. In 2020, China's military budget was $178 billion (approximately 20 percent of US spending). In 2026, their budget was over $273 billion. The president did not see the Chinese military expansion as a threat; he believed they needed to increase their military to protect their trade routes from the growing threat of pirates. He also claimed the Chinese were relieving America of some of their defense responsibilities around the globe.

China began expanding the historic silk routes to the West to promote its exports. Those efforts required the Chinese military to broaden their defenses of the region, requiring the US military to dedicate more resources to the areas by shifting them from other priorities worldwide. In 2026, the US military budget for operations exceeded $1 trillion, plus additional funds for unplanned military actions. These unexpected expenses had been significant over the past 25 years, adding directly to annual deficits in the federal budget.

Over those same 25 years, China's air transport company (COMAC) quickly grew into a worldwide presence. In 2026, they were ready to become a major competitor at the Paris Airshow. Boeing and Airbus were still recovering from some bad financial years and were targeting the Paris Airshow to increase their international sales. However, COMAC was a state-supported company that produced various aircraft that competed in the world market.

Aviation experts believed Boeing erred by allowing China to build commercial airline wings. Boeing should have realized that China would reverse engineer the wings for use in their commercial aircraft just as they did similar actions with other US companies. It was a decision Boeing executives regretted.

In 2025, Boeing and Airbus more or less evenly split $14.5 billion in new aircraft sales at the Paris Airshow. In 2026, however, COMAC's entry into the competition yielded them $4.7 billion in commercial aircraft sales, leaving $11.5 billion in sales to be split by Boeing and Airbus. This reduction in sales by the two legacy manufacturers dramatically impacted their already weak balance sheets.

The federal government spent $398 billion supporting America's welfare program in 2025. Including Medicare, the costs were $832 billion. Due to changing qualification rules, expenses increased above expectations for the last four years. The number of welfare recipients continued to grow much faster than expected. State welfare spending was $1.4 trillion. The combined incremental contributions of the federal, state, and local governments to the welfare system had doubled the inflation rate for over ten years. Projections of future payments would be substantially exceeded most years.

Climate experts claimed western states were in drought conditions eight of the previous ten years. Their opponents argued the excessive use of water was to blame, not the lack of rain. Either way, the result was annual wildfires across western states. The unbudgeted cost associated with the fires rose steadily from $24 billion in 2019 to over $83 billion in 2026. Solutions that were acceptable to environmentalists remained elusive, generating a lot of news coverage and legislative bickering but no relief.

With nearly $5 trillion in revenue, the US Treasury issued $4.7 trillion in debt in 2026. The interest rate on the issue was 4.6 percent. Foreign ownership of US debt increased to 37 percent. The largest foreign investors were China and Japan. China purchased 21 percent of the issues, increasing their total US debt to 17 percent. Japan's ownership percentage remained steady at five percent.

The federal debt at the end of 2025 was $40.7 trillion. With a budget proposal to ensure another $4.09 trillion scheduled for 2026, it required an increase in the debt limit of the United States again. The US ended 2026 with $45.4 trillion in debt.

2027

EVEN THOUGH IT had only been a year since my transfer to the computer technology sharing department in the Dallas office, I received a promotion to managing director of the department. My job was to oversee strategically crucial projects to improve the company's IT infrastructure and act as a business manager for its other IT departments. I still traveled frequently to China and Washington D.C., as before.

One afternoon, while rushing through the Dallas/Fort Worth Airport to catch a flight to Beijing, I suddenly had an eerie feeling that someone not far behind me was hurrying along the same path through the airport. "A ridiculous thought," I told myself, but I couldn't shake a sense of dread that passed through me like a sonic wave. I awkwardly turned around while still walking but did not see anyone directly behind me. There was only a woman pushing a child in a stroller on the right and two American Airlines flight attendants on the left. At work, I dealt with sensitive material that made me feel I could be the target of corporate raiders or a mark for government espionage. That paranoia to this point had always been unfounded.

* * *

CALIFORNIA HAD LONG neglected much-needed infrastructure projects. The governor pushed the state legislature to issue $800 billion in bonds to fund multiple projects. Nearly 60 percent of the bonds financed extensive improvements to the international airports in Los Angeles, San Francisco, Oakland, Sacramento, and San Diego. The rest updated the seaports of San Diego, Long Beach, and San Francisco. The bonds were purchased primarily by foreign investors/governments, with China buying 70 percent of the bond issue. Because the bonds had a provision of ownership if California defaulted, lawyers litigated anti-trust concerns in the issuer's favor. Later, an additional

$400 billion in bonds became available to address railroad terminals and tracks. The list of investors remained unchanged.

Military spending continued to increase by two to three times that of inflation as China increased its worldwide reach. The US Army added two new divisions and stationed them near the beginning and end of the new Silk Trade routes. There were no countries along the route willing to allow US troops to be within their borders. The US also added two fighter wings and an air-refueling squadron to coincide with the divisions, providing a US presence to help support any potential military action. These increased US divisions and Air Force assets were not in the budget. They spearheaded exhaustive debates in Congress during the deliberation of the next budget.

In early September, the Gulf Coast braced for Hurricane Russell. The federal government spent $13 billion preparing for the storm. They repositioned water and food rations close to the projected impacted areas. Medical supplies augmented all hospitals in the Florida panhandle and Southern Georgia, Alabama, Mississippi, and Louisiana. Public works personnel and equipment were pre-positioned to re-establish electrical services, clear and repair roads, and reconnect communication services. Emergency shelters were moved closer and readied. The US Naval Ship *USS Comfort* was positioned to the Gulf of Mexico to be ready for deployment after the storm landed.

The category four hurricane made landfall 10 miles east of Panama City, Florida, with sustained winds of 150 knots. The majority of the rain was to the northeast of the epicenter around Tallahassee, resulting in massive flooding of Florida's state capital. The total damage was $210 billion, most of which was flood and wind damage. Federal, state, and local governments were well-positioned for the storm's fallout. Medical services were, for the most part, prepared.

When the polls closed on the midterm elections, the Democrats had a 52 to 47 majority with one liberal-leaning Independent in the Senate. They strengthened their hold in the House of Representatives to 252 Democrats, 183 Republicans. The newly appointed Senate majority leader was 72 years old. He had been in the Senate since 1998 and strongly supported the president's campaign.

In the last few years, the Supreme Court reflected the heavy influence of the conservative justices appointed during the previous Republican presidency. However, in 2026, an opportunity arose for the Democratic president to fill two new Supreme Court seats with associate justices. The Republicans were unable to stop the administration from adding the new seats. Democrats believed 11 justices could better serve America's needs. Republicans furiously fought the addition. With control of both houses of Congress and the presidency, Democrats added two liberal judges to the court. Although the chief justice was appointed by a Republican president, his rulings tended to be liberal. Therefore, the new justices changing the court's 5 to 4 conservative-slant to a 6 to 5 liberal-leaning high court. Republicans had few resources available to prevent the move and could only complain bitterly to the press. Most press outlets supported the move to increase the size of the court as they opposed many of the decisions in recent rulings.

The US government had just over $5 trillion in total revenue that year. The federal debt at the end of 2026 was $45.3 trillion, with $2.4 trillion additional debt scheduled for 2027. This budget required an increase in the United States' debt limit again, now becoming an annual event. The US government debt at the end of 2027 was $49.5 trillion.

2028

I BECAME FRIENDLY with an accountant in my company's finance department in the Dallas office. We had worked together for several years, but when we started having lunch and dinner meetings, instead of working in one of the company's conference rooms, we began sharing our personal experiences, backgrounds, and hopes for the future. It turned out my colleague was born in Texas to Chinese parents.

We began traveling together on some of my trips to China. It helped to lighten my work-related anxiety and gave my work colleague additional opportunities to visit family members in Beijing.

Professionally, it gave my coworker more visibility within the Beijing office. It was a good relationship between us that was beneficial at work and growing to have social rewards.

At the urging of my company bosses, I became active in the Dallas area community. I volunteered at organizations that focused on data literacy and projects that offered support to people in need of health, education, and housing services. I was especially interested in organizations that brought STEM (Science, Technology, Engineering, and Mathematics) programs to children in underserved communities. I participated in their school programs and donated money. It was the beginning of my networking with political contacts as well.

Although I didn't serve in the US military, I donated annually to the local Veterans of Foreign Wars (VFW) and American Legion. I appreciated the opportunities I had and still have in this country and wanted to support the veterans who protected that freedom.

I was taken aback by a recent Gallup survey of attitudes about US military spending. It reported that the percentage of Americans believing the federal government was spending too little on the military fell to 21 percent in 2027 from 37 percent in 2020, greatly concerning me. Our military needed to remain the best equipped, trained, and sophisticated in the world. Our defense readiness was a powerful deterrence to our enemies worldwide and a constant reminder of our global leadership role. Many of the youth questioned the US leadership status. Our adversaries also voiced concern about our use of power to "bully" foreign nations to our needs. Now, especially in a tech-dominated environment, threats could morph quickly from the battlefield to cyberspace, and our military needed the ability to adapt immediately and counter those threats. However, the political and international pressure had many legislators pushing back on the military budget.

* * *

THE PRESIDENTIAL ELECTION of 2028 pitted a popular incumbent Democrat president against the Republican governor from Oklahoma, who had no national leadership experience. The campaign became negative in August as soon as the Republican governor received the nomination. He painted the president as a tax-and-spend liberal with low moral standards, ready to take away everybody's guns. The president claimed his challenger was a heartless racist who would kill jobs and take away people's safety net if elected. It looked and sounded like every other presidential election in the last 40 years, only a little nastier. It seemed that each year the political parties got better at being vicious.

In the end, the incumbent liberal president won. It became apparent the country was continuing to become more liberal. Historically, the country trended 40 percent conservative, 40 percent liberal, and 20 percent independent. The recent election implied the country was 55 percent liberal, 30 percent conservative, and 15 percent independent. The incumbent president won with 356 electoral votes to 182 for the Republican.

With a new mandate and both houses of Congress and the Supreme Court in Democratic control, the president pushed to fulfill his campaign promise to pass a national minimum wage of $17/hour to match the minimum wage for federal jobs and contracts. The bill made it through both houses of Congress without Republican support. The opposition claimed it would hurt small businesses and increase unemployment, but no one listened. The president signed the bill with an effective date of June 1, 2028.

The Airbus 380, the largest passenger aircraft ever built, proved to be too expensive and inefficient for most airlines to keep in service. The planes were being retired quickly. When one of the last Airbus 380s was landing south on runway 10L at San Francisco International Airport, it crashed into the terminal building. The crash killed all 524 passengers and crew aboard the plane and 415 people in the passenger terminal. The accident closed Terminals D, E, and F.

The loss of the aircraft cost the insurance company over $500 million. The repair costs of the terminals were over $17 billion, and the airport closure resulted in a $1 billion loss in revenue for the city and county of San Francisco each month. This reduction in income put pressure on the area's funding for social services and operating budgets. The city's credit rating went down based on their high debt burden, so the cost of issuing bonds meant higher interest that further strained their budget. The federal government paid $20 billion to help rebuild the terminals, but the accident was a painful event for the victims, their families and friends, the airline, the city, and the state.

In 2028, US military spending increased at three times the rate of inflation. Inflation was rising due to the US government's increased debt and corresponding interest payments. The cost of expensive new weapons, combined with protecting additional East Asian and Middle European regions from growing threats from China, amplified US military spending. Since tax revenue was not rising fast enough to cover the increased costs, it further increased government debt.

Although China had a well-deserved reputation for collecting intellectual property from numerous countries, it continued denying the allegations. Because of China's continued economic growth and burgeoning international commerce, some companies were still moving production of technically sensitive items to the People's Republic of China. The Chinese government threatened to close off the Chinese markets to companies that did not agree to build factories in China. For companies who did, China helped fund their expansion, which increased China's ownership in the parent companies.

The US federal government issued $3.1 trillion in bonds to fund government operations, with an interest rate of 4.8 percent, a five percent increase over 2027. Congress increased the US debt limit by $10 trillion to head off continued legislative battles. The process was frequent and becoming routine. By raising the limit substantially, Congress hoped to put the subject on the back burner for a few years. Unfortunately, the increased debt ceiling inspired legislators to increase spending. Foreign investors again bought the majority of the bonds offered.

In the previous 20 years, the number of earthquakes in the central United States had increased dramatically. Environmentalists claimed fracking in the early 2020s had weakened much of the land above the areas where it occurred. These weaknesses were causing permanent harm to the

Midwest. The number and intensity of the quakes increased. Oil companies refuted the claims, saying fracking was safe and allowed removing the oil without scaring the landscape or causing structural damage to the earth's crust.

Minor earthquakes significantly increased in Oklahoma and northern Texas since the oil industry expanded in the region. The practice was to reduce US dependence on foreign energy, which was successful. Since 2019, the US had been energy independent, mainly because of large-scale fracking. Although Democrats opposed fracking for many years, they hadn't had the political backing to reduce or eliminate the practice until they regained political power in 2021.

In August of 2028, a significant earthquake hit just outside of Ponca City, Oklahoma, measuring 7.4 on the Richter Scale. People felt the shock as far away as Dallas. Because of the relatively remote location of the epicenter, there were few deaths, but there was sizable damage to Ponca City and smaller communities in the area. This earthquake solidified the opponents of fracking and gained support in Congress. By the end of 2028, a bill circulated through Congress to repair the damage to the environment and eliminate future fracking. The bill had a cost of $1 trillion, plus the lost oil revenue. America's energy independence was over.

Spending far outpaced the $5.21 trillion in national income for the year. The federal debt at the end of 2027 was $49.5 trillion, with a budget to ensure another $2.6 trillion scheduled for 2028 without considering any natural disasters or unexpected military charges. With the significant increase in the debt ceiling, there was no need for additional increases. The total debt at the end of 2028 was $54.4 trillion.

2029

I WAS NOT being challenged enough at work and started looking at the possibility of running for Congress in 2030. Although I received a fantastic salary, I could not suppress my desire to work to better my own country rather than on China's behalf.

I knew that the US was approaching a critical juncture in its history. I wanted to join the fight against the decades-long expansion of a federal regime that ignored America's traditional values. In particular, to put the brakes on the out-of-control deficit spending that jeopardized the country's financial infrastructure and the institutions that held our society together. I wondered what kind of impact I could have amidst the ranks of seasoned Republicans. Yet, I strongly felt that I should try.

I set up an informal exploratory committee to test the waters to make a bid for the 3rd District congressional seat in Texas. It enabled us to start raising money for activities like polling and outreach. We were able to do this under the radar without filing reports with the Federal Election Committee (FEC) until we engaged in an official bid for the office. That would come about by referring to me as a candidate or raising more money than was reasonably needed for the exploratory activities.

My support network began with some of my University of Texas political colleagues and a few of my father's business acquaintances. My platform addressed the top issues of concern to Texans: the government had taken many of our personal freedoms; now they're trying to take away our guns; we need stricter legal immigration laws and enforcement; I'm committed to lowering taxes, reducing federal regulations, and shrinking government. My campaign slogan was, "Let's Wright the Ship."

I met with some of my politically connected colleagues. They put me in touch with the local head of the Republican party. After discussing my ideas and sketching out a rough plan, the chief of the party advised me to establish an exploratory committee to quietly judge my prospects. Since I already had an informal committee, making it official was not much of a leap. I recruited some experienced political operatives, mainly from Texas. I did include a few national personnel to address fundraising and support from other high-profile legislators. The team was positive about my prospects. I had a good fundraising network with my business contacts, and the national people believed they could help optimize my media buys. They thought we could exploit social media around my wholesome background and their perception of my good looks.

Within weeks of me deciding to become active in the Texas Republican Party, the congresswoman representing my district in Dallas announced that she would not run for re-election. Despite having no track record, I immediately began planning to run for the US Congress in 2030.

I did not like the direction our government was leading America. I wanted to get more involved and influence the future of my country. I believed the government took too many freedoms away, and I strongly supported law-abiding citizens' gun rights. The outgoing congresswoman wanted to spend more time with her family and help with her daughter's newborn, who had Down's Syndrome. Because she was not running for re-election, I consulted her about district policy goals, fundraising, and what influential people were essential to court. I also lobbied for her endorsement. At the end of our long lunch, I received her blessing. With the inputs and encouragement from my exploratory committee and the support of the outgoing representative, I decided now was the time to run for Congress.

My first priority was to pick a staff that could best support my campaign. I had a college friend who had studied political science and successfully worked his way up the bureaucratic ladder. He had helped with a couple of successful local elections and one congressional race. He was currently the assistant chief of staff for a congressman from Fort Worth. After a brief phone call, he agreed to run my campaign. My new chief of staff tapped a member of the Republican National Committee (RNC) to run our finances and control our media buys. As our staff grew, we would split these positions.

With the core of my staff established, I directed them to start building a team within the district. It was time for me to start strengthening my relationships, and I coordinated meetings with the highest-ranking leaders I could find. There were several news outlets within my congressional district. The outgoing congresswoman was instrumental in introducing me to the right people. By and large, these meetings were productive and garnered the support of those press organizations.

Similarly, the business community was interested to know who would take the reins from the outgoing congresswoman and what their regulatory interests might be. Jesse Wright was there to ease their worries. Since my views and legislative agenda were in line with most business leaders, most of those meetings proved productive in receiving the business people's endorsements and financial support for the campaign.

Since I worked in technology, I had plenty of contacts within the computer and social media companies nationwide, but primarily in Texas. I sent e-mails and texts to some strategic allies to shore up support. They seemed thrilled at the prospect of having a potential congressman to help with their projects and hold sway over future projects/legislation. They were willing to help however they could.

My more significant priorities were to minimize taxes wherever possible, reduce regulations primarily on small businesses and Texas firms, and shrink government at all levels. I believed taxes were necessary, but the current level of taxation was slowing economic growth and hurting the US competitively worldwide. Regulations are like a tax since they increase the cost of doing business. There's an old business adage that when you decide you need to hire one person, you really need to hire two. One to help with the actual work, the other to deal with the governmental paperwork and accounting. Finally, government is just too big. It is virtually impossible to live one's life without dealing with some form of government every day. By reducing taxes and regulation, the friction of doing business becomes diminished, and America prospers.

* * *

THE DOW JONES Industrial Index began the year sluggish and then continued on a downturn. Many conservatives blamed the weakness on the new national minimum wage enacted by the president. An unusual number of small businesses had closed, and the trend was accelerating. Of those businesses that remained open, many had to reduce their staff. Some businesses reduced the hours of their remaining workers and demanded more of them. Most municipalities saw an increase in unemployment claims and fewer applications to start new businesses. Inflation began to rise.

Cities needed more police to protect themselves as crime escalated. Recruiting those new law enforcement officers was difficult. The quality of the applicants was significantly lower than ten years previously, requiring an uptick in training costs and disciplinary actions. These new officers also tended to be more aggressive, which resulted in poor community relations and officer firings. The legal fees and settlements for officer-related incidents also increased dramatically. Municipalities felt the strain of funding the increased costs to keep their police force adequately staffed.

When the Fracking Correction Bill left committee, the president signed it. Energy companies' stock prices fell 40 percent in the next three days. Oil output slowed significantly. Most drilling stopped, causing oil companies to begin employee layoffs and preparing for an uncertain future. The cost of oil began to rise as oil contracts with other nations took effect to make up for the shortfall at home. The price per barrel climbed. These issues did not affect foreign countries not bound by US law. Because we had curtailed our oil production, US entities sought to fill their oil needs, but the prices carried a premium. Rising fuel costs caused the price of all consumer commodities to climb.

Coal could produce gasoline but at a much higher cost. With the pressure on the oil industry's ability to meet US needs, research into making coal conversion cheap increased. Unfortunately, the coal industry was under attack as well. The production and burning of coal produced a disproportionate amount of greenhouse gases, and mitigation to meet regulatory demands was expensive. Environmental groups lobbied lawmakers to wean America off its need for coal. Congresspersons and senators were not receptive to increased coal production as many of them were in favor of green energy and pushed for increased renewable subsidies. It inevitably meant increased costs and reduced production, resulting in oil shortages across the nation.

As hurricane season intensified in late summer, the Federal Emergency Management Agency (FEMA) and other emergency response organizations prepared. The first major storm of the year was Hurricane Bart. The projected track was up the east coast of Florida and then to Georgia and the Carolinas. The storm intensified to a category five storm, but it slowed to a category three with sustained winds of 115 knots as it approached the coast.

This storm stayed primarily over water, and its intensity remained high as it covered a large swath of land, causing substantial damage. The total cost of prep and recovery was over $263 billion. Because natural disasters were regularly occurring events, the federal government included funding in its annual budget. By 2029, the federal budget had just under $22 billion earmarked for disaster relief. The remaining $241 billion and funds for wildfires in the west, earthquakes, and tornadoes were not in the budget and required more debt.

The federal debt at the end of 2028 was $54.4 trillion. That was ten times the government's annual revenue of $5.34 trillion. With a budget to ensure another $1.5 trillion scheduled for 2029, the total debt at the end of 2029 was $59.9 trillion without a contingency for unexpected expenses or continued military actions in the Middle East.

2030

WITHIN A SHORT time, my campaign received a flood of contributions at the $2,700 limit for pre-election donors. This triggered my official candidacy far sooner than expected, which meant we had to register with the Federal Election Commission (FEC) and start filing regular financial reports. Fortunately, my significant other managed to secure a transfer from the company's Beijing headquarters to its Dallas office and took charge of managing the committee's finances and filing the FEC reports. It took a tremendous burden off my shoulders having someone I trusted implicitly in such a vital role.

Republican power brokers, along with the state and national media, took an interest in me and my campaign. The National Republican Congressional Committee (RNCC) contributed money and assigned operatives to help with travel planning, media buys, and speech writing. Because of their efforts, my speeches received significant viewing on YouTube. Also, my Twitter following was growing steadily. My message and timing were perfect. My fellow Texans were listening to what I had to say and responding favorably.

As a congressional candidate, I received significant contributions from major corporations that had moved from California to Texas. Those companies appreciated the reduced taxes and wanted to keep them that way. They saw my candidacy as a good opportunity cost for their company. I would try to make their trust warranted.

When my campaign for the 3rd District's congressional seat began, the early polls showed me lagging behind my opponent. My Democratic opponent had better name recognition, but my pledge to "Wright the Ship" and my political stances on protecting gun rights resonated with the people in my district. With recent increases in several high-profile taxes, minimizing future tax increases was making an impact. I also supported a strong military but opposed its continued use in ill-defined limitless missions. That included bringing the majority of troops from Korea and Europe home. This position was not popular with some of my Republican colleagues, but the people in Dallas loved the idea. These stances soon moved me up in the polls.

By election day, I had closed the gap. My opponent did not react quickly or decisively enough to stop my momentum. With a last-minute media push and continued social media pressure, I further pressured my opponent. The efforts yielded me a win for Texas' 3rd congressional district with barely a one percent margin - surely not a strong mandate, but a win nonetheless.

My better half resigned from the financial analyst position with the Chinese company and planned to join me in Washington DC in January of 2031. Washington DC is worlds apart from Plano, Texas. The cost of living was ridiculous since our two-bedroom apartment costs more per month than our house in Texas. There were few parks not overrun with tourists or the homeless.

Alas, the security in every building was depressing. I know things changed after the attacks of September 11, 2001, but I had hoped that eventually, there would be a return to normalcy. I had always believed the further away the government is from the governed, the more likely there would be corruption. In recent years, that seemed confirmed, but we were here to make a change.

* * *

AFTER THE PRESIDENTIAL Inauguration in January 2029, the contentiousness of the campaign subsided, and the Democratic government began to put its plans into action. The president lobbied to make Washington, DC, a state. Due to the political make-up of the city, both sides were confident Washington, DC's statehood would result in two permanent Democratic senators and one Democratic congressman. There was considerable Republican pushback on the proposal, but there was little groundswell or mainstream media coverage of the opposition. The president was the first commander-in-chief to welcome a new state to the union since Dwight D. Eisenhower did so over 70 years before in 1959. Hawaii was no longer the youngest state.

The Dow Jones Industrial Index continued its downturn. The trajectory was not a steady decline, but the trend was clear. Many conservatives blamed the new national tax policies enacted by the president. Small businesses continued to close, and the pace of closure was quickening. The oppressive taxes were beginning to affect larger companies. They could raise their prices, and they did, but they combined it with layoffs and store closures.

Most municipalities saw an increase in unemployment claims and fewer applications to start new businesses. The ripple effect of closed companies led to collateral damage affecting other companies in the area. This increased costs to both business and local governments. More police were needed to protect US cities as crime increased. The reduced number of business start-ups combined with closures had reduced customer options in many municipalities. This reduced economic activity, thus negatively affecting a municipality's ability to raise revenue to address these issues.

Although the Democrats increased their majority in the House of Representatives by four seats, a district in north Texas just outside Dallas, in the town of Plano, had added a new Republican to the mix – the newly minted Representative, Jesse Wright.

In the US Senate, the liberals also increased their majority to 56 Democrats, with 46 Republican senators. As expected, the two new senators from the State of Washington DC were Democrats without significant competition from the Republicans in the general election.

The mid-term elections of 2030 had focused heavily on the increasing costs for college. Students complained that while previous college debt had been eliminated, they were amassing substantial loans for their degrees. They wanted their four-year degree to be free or at least a guarantee that upon graduation, their loans would receive forgiveness.

They believed their argument was sound since the government forgave the previous debt, even for the students who failed to graduate. If the federal government dismissed $75,000 of student debt for each graduate, it would cost nearly $2 trillion. If the students who did not graduate were part of the total, the cost would climb to just over $3 trillion. Plus, 9.5 percent of students had more than $75,000 in debt, so they would still have loan payments. Nearly four percent of students had over $150,000 in debt. The Republicans contended that it was inappropriate to ask plumbers, electricians, and construction workers who did not attend college to pay for other students to get degrees that might not lead to gainful employment upon graduation. Again, the conservatives lost the debate, and college graduates began getting their debt forgiven when they finished college, with or without a degree.

Due to historic government subsidies, educational costs had risen at three times the rate of inflation. Opponents believed the price would grow even faster with increased government aid. Historically, subsidized programs substantially outpaced inflation: healthcare, housing, education, and rail transportation.

One of the conservative Supreme Court justices died. The president began floating the names of potential successors. The Republicans protested the liberal slant of all the names on the list. Conservatives believed the death of a conservative justice should dictate a conservative replacement. Democrats argued that there was no precedent for such consideration. The president, the majority in Congress, and the media did not see the appointment of a conservative justice as being in the best interest of the American people. The Senate hearings were quick, and the Democrats ran roughshod over the Republicans who questioned the nominee. With the full support of the Democratic Senate, they approved the president's selection of a liberal judge within days of his nomination. The court then had seven liberal judges and four conservatives.

The Chinese increasingly funded the growing US debt. Because their economy continued to grow, they believed they had financial and strategic reasons for buying US bonds. The Chinese were heavily investing in their military and pushing to make the yuan the world currency. None of this was good for America.

The government began the 2030 Census by establishing a website and encouraging citizens to complete the form online. The process was substantially cheaper than having census personnel visit every household. The problem of counting the homeless and undocumented immigrants was again problematic. Historically, the Democrats believed these demographics were under-reported, whereas Republicans believed the process produced a fair count.

A debate arose over a sampling process rather than actually counting people. Proponents of sampling believed it was more accurate and cost-effective than counting every person. In contrast, the supporters of a total headcount referenced the Constitution as preventing sampling. They also believed the sampling method was inaccurate and political. As with other scientific studies, sampling would vary depending on the variables used in the sampling selection formula. Those variables could have political slants that made the results palatable to the party in power at the time of the census. The Democrats wanted sampling, so legislation went to the House of Representatives and the Senate. The bills passed both houses on partisan votes. No Republicans voted to support the legislation. Once the conference committee reconciled the differences, both houses voted to pass the bill—again on party lines. The president signed the bill into law. For the first time in 250 years, statistical sampling governed the census rather than a direct headcount as directed by Article 1, Section 2 of the United States Constitution.

The results of the census also determined congressional representation. With the completion of the census, the political parties began gerrymandering districts to increase their party's chances of winning. The 2020 Census resulted in a reduction of representation in historically Democratic states like California and New York. With the 2030 census, the Democrats in power wanted to control the results to help strengthen their dominance in government. The use of sampling increase their ability to inflate the counts of homeless and undocumented immigrants.

Again this year, the west coast of the US had an unusual number of wildfires, most of them started by lightning. California, Oregon, and Washington were unprepared for the forest fires even though they were becoming routine. Those states requested federal resources.

The National Guard and firefighting resources from nearby states were mobilized and went in to combat the fires. In total, 4,964,366 acres burned. Most of it was in Alaska, primarily in remote areas. California (273,148 acres), Oregon (82,732 acres), and Washington (176,742 acres) had the costliest fires. In the three contiguous west coast states, the fires destroyed thousands of structures, breached transportation venues, and ruined businesses. The most expensive fires were by far in California, with the total losses topping $35 billion.

Nationally, over 23 percent of the population was over 65. Social Security benefits costs were climbing quickly, with fewer young workers funding the growth. The percentage of payroll taxes collected rose from 12.4 percent (6.2 percent each from the employee and employer) to 14.2 percent for incomes up to $137,700 (changed to $154,000 in 2025). Although legislators expected the changes to fulfill Social Security benefits obligation for twenty years, the fund needed additional revenue only five years later.

Because the population was aging, healthcare costs climbed disproportionately. Elderly citizens required more medical attention than younger ones. A Medicare tax of 2.9 percent split between employee and employer covered the cost. For high-income earners who made over $200,000 annually, an additional 0.9 percent tax went to the employee to pay. In total, the federal government was spending $1.8 trillion annually to cover Medicare, Medicaid, Veterans benefits, and the Affordable Care Act (ACA) subsidies. These costs had risen 54 percent in the last ten years.

To address these costs, the Medicare tax increased to 3.4 percent for all taxpayers, and high-income earners had an additional 1.8 percent taken for those making over $150,000. The federal government took steps to reduce costs by restricting some treatments for patients who would receive a minimal benefit due to age or infirmity. These changes received little media coverage;

they were a move toward Medicare-for-all, which liberal politicians had promised for years.

These tax increases were combined with additional public insurance options to help control costs. Although citizens were not required to transition to public sector insurance, the private sector reacted as they did in 2011, shortly after the Affordable Care Act went into effect. Private employers canceled employee healthcare and told workers to sign up for the public insurance options, taking a tremendous burden off private employers in 2011 and again in 2030.

The federal debt at the end of 2030 was $65.9 trillion, with a budget to ensure another $2.6 trillion scheduled for 2031 on revenue of $5.47 trillion, without considering any outlying factors.

2031

AFTER BEING SWORN in, we went to my new office. Although I was the junior congressman, I was impressed with the accommodations. My campaign manager became my chief of staff and had the office next to me. He was the only person with direct access to my office. There were already piles of documents on his desk that needed addressing. I'm sure I would have the chance to read most of them myself, but I had other priorities for now.

I made an appointment to consult with the Republican congressional leader at his earliest convenience. I wanted to see what committees needed a new member. The meeting was for early the following week. My next few days were filled with social gatherings and meetings to learn proper House protocol. It was an excellent opportunity to meet my fellow freshmen congresspersons and exchange our platform agendas.

When the minority leader met with me, and after the niceties, he recommended the Foreign Affairs Committee, which addressed the political relationships between the US and other countries, including resolutions and legislative measures directed to such relations. He felt my familiarity with China's policies and culture and my list of Asian contacts were sufficient to qualify me for the committee.

The leader then suggested either of two subcommittees. The first was the Asia, Pacific, and Nonproliferation, a subcommittee of the Foreign Affairs Committee with regional jurisdiction that matched my life experience. The second was the Oversight and Investigations subcommittee which fell under the House Committee on Energy and Commerce. This subcommittee conducts investigations within the jurisdiction of the controlling committee. The subcommittees have jurisdiction over legislation regarding region or country-specific loans or other financial relations outside the Foreign Assistance Act. The committee was to develop options for meeting future challenges related to U.S. interests in the region, including terrorism and cyber concerns.

I asked to be on the Armed Services Committee because of my strong support for our military. The minority leader said he had more senior members on the committee, and they all had served in the military. I would need much more seniority to overcome my lack of military service before leadership would consider me for Armed Services.

The leader also recommended me for the Judiciary Committee. Even though I'm not a lawyer, my negotiation efforts on behalf of my former Chinese employer were common knowledge in political circles as a significant contribution to minimizing US legal action against China. The minority leader believed that ability could be of use to the chairman of the Judiciary.

My next choice was the Commerce, Science, and Transportation Committee. My technology background and experience in foreign relations made this committee a good fit. After a few questions, I convinced the leader I would add value to the committee.

The Finance Committee also interested me. The minority leader felt my background in technology and recent knowledge of the financial workings of China's business sector supported this committee appointment. My Stanford Executive MBA further supported the appointment.

In the end, the leader recommended my membership in both the Asia, Pacific, and Nonproliferation subcommittee, as well as the Oversight and Investigations subcommittee. He also supported the Finance and Foreign Affairs Committees. In a rare circumstance, the leader recommended a third committee - Judiciary. After a short discussion, the Republican Conference approved me to all three committees and the two subcommittees.

The House Judiciary Committee was my favorite. It focused on protecting Constitutional freedoms and civil liberties, oversight of the Departments of Justice and Homeland Security, and addressing regulatory issues and immigration reform. Judiciary has jurisdiction over all proposed amendments to the Constitution and sent the most bills to the House floor every year. It's a very active committee that concentrates on issues that matter to me. I was lucky to get the assignment since the rest of the committee were significantly more senior congresspeople.

I know a congressman's salary seems high compared to the average income of the rest of the country, but $275,000 was insufficient to make ends meet to maintain residences in Plano and Washington, D.C. This problem was made more difficult with only one paycheck. As usual, I relied on my sweetheart to manage our personal finances, which held little interest for me despite my MBA. We kept our house in Plano. It was home and gave us a sense of stability. We rented an apartment in Washington that was much smaller than you would expect for a congressman. It was a tiny one-bedroom/one-bathroom apartment on the fourth floor of an old brownstone building with no elevator. Even though it was small, it was more expensive than our house in Texas.

We finally decided to get married. It was a small, low-key ceremony in Plano, attended by our families and a few of our closest friends. With little time for a honeymoon, we settled for a weekend in Niagara Falls before I needed to return to Washington DC. We were happy.

In addition to our dual home situation, we decided to start a family. The added costs of a baby made the expense of maintaining the Plano home impractical. As much as we hated leaving the house, we needed to downsize. We ended up selling the property and moved to a small apartment with combined office-living space in town. The monthly saving helped maintain our D.C. apartment. We now lived in two apartments.

Some of my Republican colleagues regarded me as a future golden boy of the party. Rather than letting my ego be flattered, I used their high expectations to fuel my passion for accomplishing my long-term goal to build a strong resistance coalition within the Republican Party. I felt someone needed to take the reins and lead a movement to tamp down the perilous thinking and change the direction that was spinning our government fiscally out of control. Someone had to convince voters that the consequences of chronic deficit spending endangered the future viability of our country. Voters needed to understand that the high costs of federal healthcare and social programs had put our country on the road to financial unsustainability.

* * *

ONE EVENING IN March, five F3 Tornadoes touched down in Fort Worth, Texas. Miraculously only two people were killed, but more than $3 billion in damage to the city occurred, with over 500 homes destroyed. One of the tornadoes was in nearby Arlington, doing significant damage to the joint-use airport. The east side was used for general aviation, while the west side supported Bell's military contract operations for the V-22 Osprey. The Dallas/Fort Worth Metroplex needed federal help to coordinate and rebuild their community.

To fund his domestic spending increases, the president informed the chairman of the Joint Chiefs of Staff that he planned to cut the military budget by eight percent. That freed up nearly $100 billion and reduced the Department of Defense budget to $1.1 trillion. The Joint Chiefs pushed the president to keep the budget unchanged. They claimed the reductions would affect readiness in the Middle East as we continued with our 30-year presence in the region. They emphasized the increased threat of domestic terrorism. The chiefs also voiced concern about China's continued military build-up in Asia and eastern Europe to protect their trade network. They had serious concerns about long-term readiness, as any new weapon system acquisition would be delayed or stopped by the military budget cuts. The president empathized with them but said the cuts were necessary. The military had been overfunded for far too long for it to continue.

The president had other problems as well. The latest national polls showed that Americans overwhelmingly wanted increases in their healthcare, education, and housing subsidies. He did not want to confront additional debt-ceiling debates so soon after having strong-armed Congress for a $10 trillion budget increase. The president stood his ground and cut the military budget while increasing the payments for social programs.

In September, a category one hurricane was tracking toward the Gulf coast. Although it was a relatively weak storm, FEMA and other emergency response organizations saw fit to mobilize their resources. This increased government and private sector activity and cost the federal government nearly $75 billion in unfunded monies.

Congress needed to do a better job at forecasting off-budget items. Hurricanes, wildfires, and other natural disasters were common and, although unpredictable, require more accurate inclusion in the budget. However, politicians knew voters would willfully spend money after a tragedy that they were unwilling to budget for in advance.

The 2030 Census results increased congressional representation in historically Republican states. The traditional Democratic states lost significant population. As a result of the shifting demographics, the elections of 2030 showed a stronger Democratic presence in those historically Republican regions. The effect of these shifts made the Democratic National Committee (DNC) hopeful that some of the Republican districts would be in play in future elections. Due to the census results, Texas and Tennessee picked up additional congressional seats, while California lost two and New York lost one.

The majority of the US government's budget funded entitlements. Their discretionary spending only accounted for 24 percent of the total budget of $1.7 trillion. Government spending was approximately $7 trillion on $5.4 trillion in revenue. The vast majority of federal government spending was for the military and entitlement programs. That left little room for cutting the annual deficit without addressing entitlements.

Increases in social security payments drained the general fund as Americans aged. The Social Security Trust Fund was shrinking, so the federal government could not borrow from the Trust to obscure the true cost of their debt. Addressing the cost of Social Security was unpopular with voters and had routinely cost legislators their seats. That fact made it improbable that the current Congress would address the issue.

The US Treasury floated $2 trillion in government securities to fund continued operations. Because of the size of the federal debt, inflation, and concerns for the US's ability to repay the loan, interest rates on the national debt increased to 5.1 percent. Foreign investors purchased 71 percent of the securities offering, with China acquiring 58 percent or $1.16 trillion. Japan and India purchased a combined total of 13 percent. The percentage of our debt owned by foreign countries became disconcerting to the few deficit hawks remaining in Congress.

The Chinese economy continued to grow steadily. Millions of Chinese citizens transitioned from poverty to the middle class each month. Many of their agricultural workers were migrating to the cities for industrial jobs, putting a strain on their ability to grow enough food. The Chinese government began importing more of its sustenance needs while it focused on improving its agricultural output. This involved utilizing technology from the US and Europe. Questions had persisted over the years as to whether China obtained its technology ethically and legally.

China's president continued his decades-long rejection of what he called the hegemonic power structure of global commerce. He had long called for trade reforms to reflect "the more diverse range of perspectives and values in the international community," perhaps in defense of China's aggressive programs to acquire US and European patented technology. He believed the US control over so much of the world's economy was a hindrance to progress. China's continued growth in world commerce was beneficial to the underdeveloped world because they produced commodities at a much lower price, allowing more countries access to a better quality of life for their citizens.

The FBI director, testifying before the Judiciary Committee, said that his agency was pursuing more than 800 cases of suspected Chinese theft of US technology. These cases had little potential for success. Even if the courts ruled against China, there was little chance of overriding the sovereignty of China and enforcing the judgments.

The federal debt at the end of 2031 was $72.5 trillion, with a budget to ensure another $2.6 trillion scheduled for 2032, without considering any natural disasters or unexpected military charges due to our continued presence in the Middle East. Because of the ten trillion dollars increase in the debt ceiling, there was no need to raise it again. Revenue climbed slightly to $5.61 trillion.

2032

AS A NEW CONGRESSMAN, I attempted to meet and work with the Democratic majority leadership. Against the advice of the minority leader, I met with the Speaker of the House in an effort to build a relationship for potential bipartisan support for future legislation.

The speaker did not make any promises; she used political doublespeak to make me feel reassured. After the meeting, I consulted with the minority leader, who tried to explain to me how politics worked and the speaker's history. The majority leader was a seasoned politician. She promised me access and support for bipartisan legislation that met both of our goals to care for the American people. She meant she would accept my support for her legislation; I should not expect her to back my initiatives as her party would see that as weak.

As a congressman, I have to get re-elected every two years. Although I was a new congressman, I had to begin fundraising almost immediately after taking office. Even though I had yet to sponsor any successful legislation, I was very popular in my home district in Plano and also Dallas. That popularity, coupled with my extensive business contacts, helped me raise large sums of money. My re-election fight was contentious because the Democrats made a major push to unseat me. Because I was a junior congressman and had not accomplished much yet, they believed I was vulnerable. After some hard campaigning and more than a few sleepless nights, I won re-election by six percent with a low voter turn-out.

* * *

THE POPULAR DEMOCRATIC president ran for re-election against the senior senator from Texas. The senator's campaign pushed for more fiscal responsibility and a stronger national defense. The president supported domestic programs to buoy the economy and help people hurt by recent weaknesses in the economy. The president's plan to increase spending on the people was a big hit. His opponent could not get his message of fiscal responsibility and more spending on the military to resonate with voters.

As inflation rose, more people signed up for financial benefits, and the buying power of social security payments to the elderly fell significantly. The president proposed increasing social security benefits by 15 percent after three years of only marginal increases. The result was an increase of $200 billion in social security costs each year. Aging Gen-Xers and Millennials were now thinking about their retirements for the first time. Since they hadn't done much planning before, it helped the president win a lopsided victory with 395 electoral votes.

With the president winning an easy victory, Democrats who were up for re-election rode his coattails. Democrats running in districts and states held by Republicans worked at establishing or strengthening their ties to the president, who made many campaign stops in winnable districts. The result was an increased majority in both the House of Representatives (261 to 174) and one seat picked up by Democrats in the Senate (57 to 45). With strong local support, I was able to keep my place in Congress.

Mount Wrangell, 206 miles Northwest of Anchorage, began showing signs of geothermal activity in early June. In mid-July, it erupted. The eruption qualified as a large event on the Volcanic Explosivity Index, measuring a four on that scale – the equivalent of the Mount St. Helens eruption in 1980. The eruption's timing and location were troublesome. It was the height of the tourist season, and the ash cloud covered the commercial aviation routes from the lower 48 US states to Anchorage. Alaska Airlines alone had 32 flights a day from Seattle to Anchorage to feed the cruise ship industry. The ash blew southeast over the inland passage, further disrupting the tourist season for a state that relies heavily on summer cruise ships. Many cruises had to cancel to avoid the volcanic ash.

To help the state recover from the natural disaster, $250 billion went to Alaska's state government, with an additional $75 billion given to the municipalities along the inland passage for clean-up. Per capita, Alaska received more federal money annually than any other state because of the expansive road system and military presence combined with its small population. This $325 billion was in addition to their regular funding.

Due to the recent increase in entitlements and net interest payments, those two expenses alone consumed all tax revenue the US federal government received for the 2032 fiscal year. Therefore, debt financed all other costs, including the military ($1.02 trillion), veterans benefits ($260 billion), education ($160 billion), transportation ($155 billion), et al. The treasury issued $7 trillion in new debt at 5.4 percent interest. Foreign governments purchased almost all the debt.

The federal debt at the end of 2032 was $79.7 trillion. With a budget to ensure another $2.9 trillion scheduled for 2033, an increase in the debt limit was unnecessary because of the significant increase the previous year. The coffers received just $5.75 trillion in revenue.

2033

WHILE BEING SWORN in for the second time, reciting my oath of office reignited my resolve to do what was right for America. I felt quite a bit wiser about the legislative process and, therefore, a better politician, which is not a compliment in Republican circles. Even with my support for some Democratic legislation, I had no luck getting any of my legislation passed by the House.

My position advanced to senior minority member of the Judiciary Committee. Even though I was relatively junior, the other committee members believed that my experience and knowledge of global systems and politics warranted it. I was able to bring more of my issues to the committee. However, since the Democrats still ran the committee, my bills were shot down.

I introduced legislation to strengthen the protection of US intellectual property rights internationally, specifically with China. However, the committee chairman blocked the legislation from going to the floor, citing his opinion that the timing wasn't right for the bill. I saw the same thing happen multiple times to Republican-proposed legislation in my first two years in Congress. As the Democrats increased their majority in both houses, their attempts at bipartisanship faded, and Republican bills were never forwarded.

* * *

AS SOON AS the president's inauguration and the new House of Representatives and Senate members were seated, the administration began penciling out their priorities – more broadly defined infrastructure projects and an increase in Medicare and Social Security benefits. There was also a renewed interest in the US space program. In the last decade, successful collaborations with civilian aerospace companies had spurred plans for further joint space exploration beyond Mars. This collaboration helped reduce the costs of maintaining the US space agency, but all the initiatives significantly outpaced revenue.

American interest in civilian space travel had also increased. Private aerospace companies had embraced and promoted this idea since the early 2000s. Private citizens had been willing to spend large sums of money to fly in space. The marketplace was now providing that opportunity. Although the private companies bore the majority of the cost, federal and state funds subsidized the research.

Americans had grown weary of the US military's constant presence in the Middle East, which had resulted in a steady stream of Americans killed in recent years. The increased visibility of disabled troops on national television began to wear on the psyche of families with children of military age. Americans were also questioning our continued military presence in Korea, Germany, and other countries. This continued strain on America reached into political circles.

Military leaders had begun reducing non-essential forces overseas. The president used the reduction in military spending to increase the budget for space exploration, which amounted to only a drop in the bucket. Still, the president made political points for himself by promoting the concept.

Military generals addressed the effect on our defense readiness in light of the president's cuts.

Criticism of the current administration when a general retired had been common practice for decades. However, this president reminded the generals that although they *defended* freedom of speech in the military, they did not *have* freedom of speech. By speaking outside of the chain of command, they were potentially committing criminal acts even after retirement and would be held accountable. He made an example out of one four-star general. After the general retired, he participated in a news interview which was unfavorable to the administration. The president took away two stars and stripped him of his security clearance, effectively reducing his military retirement pay and devaluing him as an expert by denying him access to current information.

As new initiatives captivated the American people, higher social program costs were taking their toll. To compensate, Congress proposed reducing military spending by another 20 percent. Military leaders and congressional members with military bases in their districts fervently protested these cuts. The president's budget proposal included a three-year increase in the retirement age and Medicare eligibility to 70. He planned to increase the age immediately rather than the traditional phased-in approach. He projected the move would save the federal government $67.3 billion; the actual number was closer to $25 billion. The president also wanted to means-test social security, but the political blowback was more than Congress was willing to withstand. The president continued to push for means testing, as it was early in his term, and he would not face another election — however, this time, he lost.

After the budget cuts, military readiness showed weaknesses. Military leadership chose to significantly reduce domestic spending in favor of keeping current overseas operations funded. Domestic military bases had to delay their construction projects; new base housing projects stopped. The reduced spending on domestic bases caused increased unemployment and reduced economic activity in those congressional districts. Fewer and fewer legislators had bases in their districts, making it harder to build support for military spending.

Other base services had reduced funding: commissaries, base exchanges, and recreational services. Recruiting efforts slowed, and service members in support roles cross-trained for combat specialties. Military personnel that continued to serve spent additional time overseas away from their families. There was a direct correlation between waning morale and suicide among service members.

Even with the domestic reductions, foreign bases also felt the sting. Troop numbers diminished in Germany. In South Korea, many of the smaller bases closed. The rotation of troops to the Middle East slowed, causing more extended tours of duty and more strain on service members. There was a significant increase in the number of service member divorces and suicides in overseas locations. Re-enlistments were also very low, putting an additional strain on recruitment and training costs. The quality of the recruits was lower, increasing the cost of required training.

The US Gulf coast braced for another significant hurricane. The federal government had budgeted $25 billion for natural disasters, but the pre-hurricane logistics cost nearly $30 billion. A category one hurricane made landfall five miles east of Corpus Christi, Texas, much further west than most Atlantic storms. With winds of 80 miles per hour, nearby Houston quickly received six inches of rainfall, causing flooding. Storm damage totaled about $650 million, but the natural disaster fund was already empty, and the hurricane and wildfire seasons were just beginning.

On the diplomacy front, the president relied on sanctions and freezing foreign funds to strengthen our global support system, knowing that the spending cuts diminished our military. Alas, restricting adversaries from US markets had little effect since increasing globalization meant countries could obtain their domestic needs from other nations. If the US could not supply their needs, they would seek help from other countries. China was frequently willing to step in, further weakening US power in the military and political arenas.

America's domestic energy production was down due to the elimination of fracking, reluctance to use coal, and an unwillingness to use nuclear power. This increased the price of energy in the US at double the rate of inflation and also increased the leverage of our energy-producing adversary nations. The US practice of freezing assets of foreign rivals motivated those countries to improve their economic activities with China using the yuan instead of the US dollar. This exacerbated inflation with a flood of US currency in the marketplace combined with increased US dollar production to reduce the deficit. The combination of US energy policy and deficit spending further challenged the American government's ability to maintain a leadership position in global geopolitical relations.

In 2033, a 7.6 magnitude earthquake hit India. The quake was centered 15 miles north of New Delhi along the Himalayan frontal thrust of the Sumatra fault. Although India had made substantial improvements in its infrastructure to minimize quake destruction, the damage was extensive. The US sent $7 billion in quake relief from the Department of Defense (DOD) budget. Before recent cuts, the DOD budget had $19 billion for emergency relief. Those funds were used for the 15 to 20 projected emergencies a year. This year's budget was exhausted by 130 percent in three crises, meaning all other situations relied on unscheduled debt.

The US government issued over 7 trillion in debt, and China continued to increase the percentage of the bond issue they purchased. With increased inflation, politicians publicly condemned the reduced buying power of the US dollar. Privately, the idea of paying off strong borrowed money with weaker inflated dollars gave the politicians more leeway to increase deficit spending. Even with their complaints, their spending habits did not change.

The total debt at the end of 2033 was $87.7 trillion, with a budget to ensure another $7.97 trillion scheduled for 2034. With only $5.89 trillion in revenue, this budget required an increase in the debt limit of the United States again, as the country surpassed its significant $10 trillion increase.

2034

THE "JESSE WRIGHT" name recognition outside my congressional district in Texas had grown considerably due to aggressive support of state initiatives in the upcoming election. I strongly supported several tax-related amendments that had failed in previous political cycles. One initiative was to prohibit the legislature from enacting new taxes on securities transactions, operations, and other business-related actions. I also supported the authorization of a new political subdivision to limit the amount of taxes imposed on disabled or elderly homeowners. These changes would reduce politicians' ability to raise taxes on some of the most vulnerable Texans.

The subsequent passing of my tax-related amendments made Texas more attractive to companies looking to relocate from states with higher taxes and regulations that hindered business growth. Finally, I fought for the state judiciary to increase the eligibility requirements for a judge of the Texas Supreme Court, the Court of Criminal Appeals, and district judges. These modifications addressed changes in Texas demographics and increased access to courts.

I continued to work with state legislators to reduce regulations and taxes on businesses. The influx of people from California and New York who had followed their jobs to Texas over the last dozen years had consistently voted for increasing the social services that made their former states untenable. The result was that the problems that made their old states worthy of abandoning showed signs of manifesting themselves in Texas. I did not believe this was in the best interest of most Texans and vehemently opposed their passage.

* * *

THE BOTTOM LINE in the high-tax and over-regulated states was that the people wanted more government than they were willing to support with taxes. That forced those states to search for new sources of revenue constantly. Some politicians stressed increasing taxes on the wealthy, but the unrealistic numbers they presented would never raise the needed tax revenue. Taxes had to be raised on the middle class to meet most states' balanced budget requirements for their operating budget. However, that did not bring in enough revenue, leaving state politicians trying to find more money to bring into the coffers. Most of those new revenue sources fell lower on the socio-economic classes that could ill-afford the tax.

With the president riding a tide of popularity, the mid-term election allowed Democrats to field a strong team of candidates. The Republicans lost the four close races they had hoped would reduce the Democrat's stronghold on Congress. In the end, Democrats picked up those four seats to make their majority 265 to 170. The Republicans also lost a Senate seat in Wyoming to increase the liberal's majority 58 to 44. This term would continue the solid one-party hold of government in Washington, DC.

In June of 2034, one of the conservative justices on the US Supreme Court was diagnosed with pancreatic cancer. With over two years remaining of the current administration's term, the associate justice, wanting to spend his remaining time with his family instead of waiting to see if the next Republican presidential candidate won, resigned. The president then nominated an ultra-liberal judge who believed that the Constitution was a living document that should change with the times. She was easily confirmed, changing the makeup of the Supreme Court to eight liberal and three conservative justices.

In Washington state, as in many other US states, the long-term degradation of infrastructure was a significant issue. In Olympia, the state legislature issued a $125 billion bond to fund substantial repairs and upgrades to the seaports of Seattle and Tacoma and SeaTac International Airport. Chinese investors purchased the majority of the bonds. Over the next five years, many states issued proportional bonds to address long-neglected infrastructure projects. Those debt issues were on top of already overstretched state budgets. Foreign investors were the overwhelming consumers of the offering.

In the past, state governments had promised public unions lucrative retirement plans, especially during election years. With the combination of those retirement plans and the anticipated sizable infrastructure expenditures, state budgets were in trouble. Although many states had balanced budget requirements covering their operating budget, they were allowed to carry debt for capital expenditures. Still, the budgets had become exorbitant, with interest payments becoming a significant part of their overall budgets. That, combined with their unfunded retirement promises, left a disturbing imbalance in their finances.

The president wanted to increase assistance to global allies and expand the list of countries receiving US aid, believing that keeping potential adversaries friendly was less expensive than military alternatives. In 2034, the US budget appropriation for foreign assistance was $57 billion, 25 percent for public health, 24 percent for humanitarian aid, and 23 percent for peace and security. The cost to administer the US foreign assistance program was $2.1 million. Conservatives believed the money could be better spent on domestic needs—but they lost. For 2035, the President proposed $70 billion for foreign assistance. After heated floor debates and a strong media push, he received $66 billion.

For the second time in three years, the president established a new cabinet position—the Department of Humanity (DOH). Its goal was to address minority and gender issues, including supporting women's promotion opportunities and pay equity. The public push was for private companies to show more substantial support for gender and minority issues. He also directed the military to increase their equity efforts as well. Democratic legislators in both houses of Congress strongly supported the new cabinet position.

With minority groups having built strong voter blocks and continually petitioning the federal government for additional benefits and protections, the DOH became the focal point for addressing these activities. The department tracked governmental proportionality of minorities and women in government jobs and attempted to influence private company hiring and placement of their represented groups in management, leadership, and board membership. Republicans claimed the move was to ensure minority and gender quotas throughout all levels of government and corporate entities. Again, the Republicans lost the battle.

If private companies were not in compliance with the DOH's hiring goals, they took legal action or implemented sanctions with marginal success. Because of this limited success, the DOH lobbied Congress to increase the legal consequences for those private companies that did not comply with the department's directives. These consequences included the loss of government contracts and financial penalties. The DOH found sympathetic ears in the halls of Congress, and the penalties stiffened.

With the previous cuts in military spending, leadership struggled to meet the needs of the services without the support of political leaders. All services reduced their training footprint to the bare essentials needed for readiness. Most generals agreed they were unsuccessful. Many units were less than 50 percent mission-ready with little hope of increasing their capability in the coming years without significant increases in funding. Military experts voiced their opinion about the degradation of military readiness as a threat to national security and reduced economic activity.

The Chinese yuan, growing in dominance for worldwide trade and reserves, caused several countries to reduce the US dollars they held. Some countries eliminated their US dollar reserves completely, resulting in an unscheduled surplus of US currency in the marketplace. This surplus caused US inflation to increase to 13.4 percent, the highest since the 1970s during the Carter Administration. By year's end, the price for a gallon of gas was $9, and a loaf of bread was $8.50. Welfare rolls and food stamp programs rose significantly, which increased the costs to state and local governments. They needed to request assistance from the federal government, which had its own funding problems and was unwilling to meet the state and municipal requests.

The US government issued $8.2 trillion in new debt, which was a considerable increase, considering there was only $6 trillion in revenue in the US treasury. Foreign investors continued to be the primary consumers of the bonds. Some countries were reluctant to buy the bonds but did not have a better option considering the increased interest of 9.2 percent paid to compensate for inflation. Many Republican lawmakers saw this level of interest as unsustainable, but they were not given a voice in Congress to address the issue.

The federal debt at the end of 2034 was $96.4 trillion with a budget to ensure another $8.7 trillion scheduled for 2035, without considering the increased cost of natural disasters or the military charges due to our continued presence in the Middle East, though that strength was at its lowest in decades. This budget required an increase in the debt limit of the United States again.

2035

I WAS STARTING to be regarded as a respected political leader by local and national media and frequently courted for speaking engagements in Texas and appearing on news shows to discuss issues or current legislation. I did my best to be worthy of the designation – a leader who was knowledgeable, trustworthy, and relatable. This increased notoriety did not increase the success rate of legislation I sponsored, but the visibility was good for my career. I asked my staff to explore the feasibility of running for the US Senate. I was a prolific fundraiser and had established contacts throughout Texas and nationally.

Some in the party tried to persuade me to run for governor of Texas. Although I was interested in the prospect of becoming governor, I knew I would have a difficult primary challenge from the aging current Republican governor. If I did win, I would have more control over the state's agenda than I would as a senator. However, I was increasingly engrossed in national politics and decided that the Senate was a better place to use my expertise toward future political growth. I discussed my choices with my family, and they were supportive of me remaining in Congress with an eye on some senior position in the future.

I worked with a ranking minority member of the Appropriations Committee to explore the possibility of increased funding for MAD Science and other STEM programs. Although many in Congress supported STEM's mission to educate more kids in science, technology, engineering, and math, the kids in those programs weren't old enough to vote. Over the last few years, funding decreased from its highest level in 2025. The two Republicans on the appropriations committee could not get support from the Democrats for increases. The motion died in committee.

* * *

HISTORICALLY, FUNDING FOR the homeless was primarily a private-sector effort. At the beginning of this century, local governments increased their efforts to work with those private organizations. By then, the cost of addressing homelessness had risen beyond the ability of private organizations and local governments to absorb. The federal government contributed $5 billion to homelessness, just 3.6 percent of total spending on the problem. State and municipal legislatures had to supply the remaining 96.4 percent.

Local governments banded together to encourage the federal government to take the burden off their shoulders, as the problem had become much more significant nationwide. In the past, the federal government disbursed funds through programs within the US Department of Housing and Urban Development (HUD), Department of Veterans Affairs (VA), Department of Education (DOE), and Department of Health and Human Services (HHS). These programs had sporadic successes but overall were deemed ineffective and underfunded. Politicians used their support of those programs to hide from the absolute responsibility of homelessness.

The president created a new Department of Homelessness, organized under HUD to centralize federal efforts to alleviate the homeless problem. The existing Continuum of Care (CoC) grant program became incorporated into the new department. The initial budget for the Department of Homelessness was $450 billion, which was a sizable increase in the federal commitment to alleviate the problem.

For 45 years, the United States had been the only superpower. The US failed to adequately respond to threats to that status over the years by the Chinese government. For decades, the Chinese stole US intellectual property. As US businesses started looking overseas to reduce costs, China saw the opportunity. It encouraged companies to bring their manufacturing to China, where the cost of labor was very low. The temptation was too great.

When American and European companies built their factories in China, Chinese officials acquired the specifications for those companies' products. The products were then knocked off and easily competed against the original goods since China did not have to recoup an investment in research and development. The Chinese government had mastered the process of tempting companies to build within China's shores.

The growth of COMAC (Commercial Aircraft Corporation of China) and their intense competition with Boeing had the most significant single-company financial impact. The theft of its patented aircraft designs cost Boeing billions of dollars in sales. Because of this situation, the

Chinese economy continued to outpace that of the US. This gave the Chinese a tremendous influence and diminished US economic strength across the globe.

The economy is not the only measure of global power. Due to budget cuts and the expanded use of military force, US military power was weakening. At the same time, the Chinese military expanded. It significantly increased its army's size to protect its massive border and expand the military support to its allies. China's air force broadened to support the growing armed forces, but the navy is what the country increased the most.

In 2020, the US had eleven naval carrier groups while the Chinese had three. By 2035, the US had ten carrier groups with seven mission ready, and the Chinese had fifteen – with three more planned for the next four years. Their aircraft carriers included increased fighter wings and support aircraft. Older aircraft carriers supported up to 40 aircraft. As the US fleet aged, the newer Chinese models carried 60 aircraft, significantly increasing the lethality of their modern aircraft carriers.

China's increased economic and military strength, combined with its recent currency maneuvers, made China the major player in geopolitical power. For the first time in the lifetime of most American citizens, the United States was not the predominant superpower on the earth.

Most American's were in denial and considered the news reports as Chinese rhetoric unsupported by facts. Politicians followed the polls and failed to react. Of course, many questioned whether the US could address the new challenges.

In New York City, an explosion on a subway train during rush hour at Grand Central Terminal killed 278 people and sent 410 more to local hospitals. It was determined to be a terrorist attack. The Transportation Security Administration (TSA) and the Department of Homeland Security (DHS) took over the investigation. Eventually, three people were arrested and convicted. The attack identified weaknesses in US transportation infrastructure. The TSA implemented additional security measures on all passenger train stations nationwide and railroad border crossings to prevent future incidents. Those infrastructure changes required $200 billion in equipment and installation costs. The additional staffing requirement added $4 billion annually to TSA's budget, plus administrative costs.

Spending on green energy had increased to nearly $3.1 trillion annually. Technological advancements had decreased the cost of green energy to $2.50 per megawatt, but the location of the producers of green energy was still problematic. Although politicians and voters liked the idea of renewable energy, they did not like the idea of windmills and solar panels near them. Since there is significant energy loss in transit, the cost of landed renewable energy was between $4 and $6 per megawatt. Because of logistical issues, the cost of renewable energy was unsuccessful at replacing oil, coal, and natural gas regardless of the decades of governmental subsidies.

The unemployment rate had been over 10 percent for the last four years. Although government officials wanted to increase employment, the US government's financial situation gave them few tools. Thus, the unemployment number stayed high. Business start-ups increased slightly but did not have the positive economic effect politicians had hoped.

High unemployment meant contributions to charities continued to decrease. At the height of charitable giving in 2019, US citizens donated $449 billion. That number sporadically reduced to less than $100 billion in 2035. Historically, US international humanitarian contributions accounted for 60 percent of total giving, but in 2035, the percentage fell to 25 percent. On both domestic and international giving, China had consistently ranked amongst the lowest contributors. Now that they were the largest economy, their lack of giving was even more significant.

Many of the smaller charities had to disband, and others consolidated. With fewer charities, the demand for government social services increased, as did the homeless problem. The reduction in private international donations caused considerable suffering for populations in developing countries, reducing the quality of life for a large portion of the world's neediest. China was the only country with the perceived resources to help. It helped its own poor as the Chinese government continued to move millions out of poverty at home.

Continued growth in followers of the Modern Monetary Theory in Congress caused a wave of increased spending. Congress voted for, and the president signed, a bill eliminating the debt ceiling. This eradication of the barrier to borrowing meant the annual political fight to raise the limit was no longer required. The elimination of the congressional debate of the debt ceiling resulted in a reduced transparency in the budgetary process. Since the media was not covering the process, few citizens or organizations could garner public outrage to limit spending. Deficits increased substantially, helping legislators in a couple of ways. They no longer had to go on record supporting the increased debt, and legislators did not need to answer budget questions while campaigning. The only ones who suffered were the American people.

This year the US government had to issue $9.6 trillion in new debt. The interest rate continued to climb to 9.7 percent to keep pace with inflation.

Foreign investors continued to be the primary buyer of the bonds. They were not enthusiastic about buying the bonds, but the increased interest plus the perceived historical lack of risk with US bonds motivated those countries, especially China. Many Republicans again voiced their concerns in Congress about the rising debt, to no avail.

The federal debt at the end of 2035 was $106 trillion, with a budget to ensure another $9.9 trillion scheduled for 2036 on revenue of $6.2 trillion.

2036

I WAS FRUSTRATED with my attempts to get grassroots support for the Republican message. With the Congress, Senate, Supreme Court, and the presidency in Democrats' hands, our issues received little to no attention from most news outlets. We were ineffective at advancing our agenda in the halls of Congress also. We tried to reach other media outlets, but Fox News was the only one giving us a voice. Our online presence did provide details of our message to our base but reaching those moderates who would be receptive was proving difficult. Most media outlets tended to support the Democrat agenda. I believe this resulted from the 24-hour a day news cycle on too many television stations, talk radio, and the internet. All of these outlets needed content to boost market share. The Democrats were always looking for problems, and their efforts resulted in producing content for the outlets. The Republicans generally believed the government should not be involved with every aspect of Americans' lives. Thus, they made less material for the ravenous media appetite. So, the media needed the liberal mindset to feed their need for material. That was why I believed most media outlets were liberal; it was in their self-interest to support the party that gave them the most content.

This preponderance of liberal media had fostered strong support of the Democrat agenda by many Americans because they had not taken advantage of the opportunity to measure both ideologies fairly against each other. I believe if the American people compared the two sides of the political issues, conservatives would win the rational debate, but that was not the world in which we lived. Conservatives needed to find a way to demonstrate why we were better for our country.

The current one-party rule allowed one ideology to grow unchecked. The Democrats could enact their belief that government could solve our citizens' problems through public programs. That policy theory resulted in high deficits that might be unsurmountable. With current federal government expenditures more than doubling annual revenue intake, the austerity measures needed to balance the budget could be more than our citizens could tolerate.

Closer to home, the Republican hold on most Texas public offices had been decreasing for years as the influx of people from high tax states had changed the demographics. This shift toward a liberal view in a historically conservative state proved challenging to me. Usually, my run for the Senate would have been a hard fight in the Republican primary since the seat had been Republican for decades. After an exhausting primary win this year, the fight had to continue as the polls showed a very tight race with my Democrat opponent. The cost of this campaign was more than all my previous runs combined.

My platform was to reduce government involvement in people's daily life and reduce regulations on business. However, a growing number of Texans wanted the government to provide more services. Honestly, promising what the populous wanted and being responsible with the state's tax dollars was becoming difficult. My opponent was stumping for continued benefits that were unrealistic with the current tax structure. After a hard-fought election, I believe my personality and resolve earned my narrow victory to become the junior senator from the great state of Texas.

All conservative candidates did not fare as well during this election cycle. The conservative candidate for governor fought a courageous battle against a charismatic and eloquent opponent. His efforts were in vain as Texans wanted what the Democratic candidate was promising. I campaigned for the losing candidate, as I could not see how the Democrat could afford all his new programs. For the first time in 42 years, Texas had a Democrat governor.

* * *

THE REPUBLICAN PRESIDENTIAL primaries began with eight candidates. There were three senators, all with great name recognition and a history of running for president. Obviously, none of them had ever won. Two congressmen were just starting to make names for themselves. They were young, sharp-looking, and articulate representatives with meteoric rises to power. There were two former department secretaries, both with long histories of public service. Since it had been a while since there was a Republican president, these men were older than the rest of the field. Finally, there was a governor. He was young and tan. He was from the great state of Florida, where he had been governor for just over one term. He was the only one in the field with any chief executive experience.

As the primaries continued, the candidates began dropping out. Two left the campaign for ethical issues around sexual misconduct, complete with pictures. The third was for financial transgressions; he had enriched himself at taxpayer expense. The youthful congressmen were not ready for the pressure of a national campaign. Finally, the governor from Florida was the last person standing. He ran on fiscal responsibility and limiting government intrusion into business—a man after my own heart.

The Democrats had fewer candidates wanting to replace the popular sitting president. With the outgoing president's support, the vice president quickly became the front runner. The other candidates realized they should drop out for the good of the party. The platform for the vice president included increased job opportunities, reduction of inner-city crime and drug use, and increased use of green energy. These issues were in line with the outgoing president's agenda.

After the conventions, the governor and vice president began changing their focus from opponents within their own parties to the opposing doctrine. The governor focused on changing the reliance on the government to encouraging individual responsibility. The vice president advocated for governmental actions to relieve individual suffering from current economic conditions. The two men did not like each other, and it showed during the debates. The governor pushed hard to show the vice president as a tax and spend liberal who would continue the deficit spending and high inflation. The buying power of Social Security checks and other fixed-income retirement programs had diminished. With private companies divesting themselves from defined benefit programs for the past fifty years, the only people with steady incomes from a retirement program were government employees with underfunded plans. The governor wanted everybody to know the vice president would continue that trajectory. The vice president pressed the governor on how he planned to reduce the deficit. He claimed the governor would devastate the social safety net that many Americans relied on during these uncertain times. Citizens went with the Democrat because they wanted to keep getting their benefits. The Democratic vice president won the election with 398 electoral votes.

In a post-election interview, the defeated governor said it was a hard-fought battle, but in the end, the people would rather have what the government offered them for free than the fruits of their labor. It was hard to beat what the Democrats were selling: free versus work.

State elections continued the steady trend. The Democrats increased their majority in both the House and Senate. They picked up three seats from southern states in the House of Representatives to make their majority 268 to 167. They increased their lead in the Senate, making the breakdown 60 to 42.

Over the past few years, the market indices had been volatile. Businesses had been growing slowly year over year, but political unrest and an influx of US dollars into the worldwide market had interfered with market performance. The vice president was happy that in this election year, the market showed modest growth. It's easier to win when the market is up, and your party is in power. Taking credit for the actions of other unaffiliated factions is a political keystone move.

Heavy rains through the Midwest caused damaging floods. Environmentalists blamed climate change. There had been two years of droughts preceding the thunderstorms that were drenching the central US, and the mighty Mississippi river was breaching its banks as the floodwaters rushed toward New Orleans. Saint Louis was the first major city ravaged by the high waters. The river was 23 feet above flood stage, and the city was not ready. Over $28.5 billion went to Saint Louis alone. Baton Rouge was the next low-lying city to sustain damage with 19 inches of rain.

Interstate 10 was closed for four days. The waters peaked as they approached New Orleans, flooding the city. People found themselves stranded on rooftops to escape. Roads closed, and emergency services strained to the breaking point. In total, the damage exceeded $217 billion.

For decades the federal government had spent substantially more money each year than it collected in tax receipts. Some academics had been advising politicians that because we made our own money and the US dollar was the world reserve currency (for now), debt is not a problem. If we felt the debt was too excessive, we could print enough money to alleviate the debt. The legislature had been using that advice to increase the budget at an alarming rate. The president, in consultation with the chairman of the Federal Reserve, decided to test the theory. Rather than print enough dollars to pay off the national debt, they would print enough to cut the 2037 deficit in half. The US government printed $4 trillion without a corresponding bond issuance. The following year, inflation skyrocketed to 32 percent.

True to form, China continued to buy US bonds. There were fewer to buy, so China had to find other securities for investment. There were governments around the world that spent more than they had in tax revenue. China just had to pick the ones with the lowest chance of default.

The federal debt at the end of 2036 was to be $106 trillion, with a budget to ensure another $8.7 trillion scheduled for 2037, without considering any natural disasters or unexpected military charges due to our continued presence in the Middle East. Revenue for the year climbed to $6.34 trillion. The actual debt at the end of 2036 was $117 trillion.

2037

MOVING MY OFFICE from the House of Representatives to the halls of the Senate was surrealistic. My office was bigger and more opulent. The dining facility served better food with more selections. Truthfully, it was probably the same, but it felt better. I had authorization for a larger staff, and after bringing my congressional staff with me, I still had jobs to fill. Finally, the halls were not as crowded. When you go from 435 representatives to 102 senators, that's a big difference. I also felt there was more visibility and responsibility to serve my country.

Once the newness wore off, it was time to find my place in this new world. I made an appointment with the Senate minority leader to see what committees he believed would fit my skills best. The leader recommended the Finance Committee because of my work in the House of Representatives. There was an opening, so that was my first assignment. Since finance is one of the super "A" committees, it was a real privilege to be assigned the post.

I suggested a place on the Appropriations Committee next, but he said he had more senior senators who wanted that job, so I had to look elsewhere. Plus, Appropriations was also a super committee, and Senate rules limited members to one "A" committee membership. He did say there was an opening on the Budget Committee. That committee usually goes to more senior members of the caucus, but the leader specifically wanted me. I was honored.

As the conversation continued, the minority leader said he could use me on the Banking, Housing, and Urban Affairs Committee, which seemed like an unusual fit for me. Still, since the minority leader selected me for the assignment, it was difficult to decline.

The next committee I wanted was Commerce, Science, and Transportation. The minority leader liked the idea. My work with international commerce in China and support of their worldwide markets made the appointment logical.

Additionally, my experience in Congress and my time working with China in the private sector gave me unique skills in dealing with international dignitaries.

As in the House of Representatives, I sought a position on the Armed Services Committee. I was a strong supporter of the military and service families. I wanted to be a part of ensuring the country treated them well and that our servicemembers received the care they needed. And like the House, I was rejected because of my lack of experience. I had never served in the armed services, and the minority leader believed he had more qualified senators who should populate that committee.

Finally, he recommended the Select Committee on Intelligence. Since I was fluent in Mandurian, he believed I would interpret Chinese communications without the intelligence community's bias. That would help the Senate make better decisions with more accurate information. Although I agreed to serve on the committee because I was not in a position to question the minority leader's judgment, it seemed my tasking would be to second guess our intelligence agencies. That would not leave me in good stead with them when I needed their help, but I would fulfill my duties to the best of my ability. I had hoped I could be of service to both sides of the debate. I could help the intelligence community if they had conflicting interpretations of the data and make the minority leader comfortable with what the intel community provided him.

A few months after being sworn in as the junior senator from Texas, I received a message from the White House. The president was planning a trip to China. Although I was a proud member of the opposition, he believed my experience working for a Chinese company that had dealings internationally was beneficial. My ability to speak Mandurian reassured him that the translators were getting the message correct in both directions. There would be delicate talks, and he did not want any misunderstandings. I agreed to go and was happy with the opportunity to visit some old colleagues—if time permitted.

When the Senate minority leader heard about the request, he was skeptical. He was concerned the exceptionally experienced politician who occupied the White House would take advantage of the new senator from Texas. After I discussed the trip and the agenda with the leader, he reluctantly agreed. He cautioned me to keep an eye on the president and his staff. If something the president did or asked felt inappropriate, he told me to walk away and call him.

The agenda for the meeting was going to be tenuous. The president wanted China to continue financing US bonds. Although our debt was high, he suggested we had a strong economy, which was political speak since our markets had dropped precipitously. We were making what could arguably be called draconian cuts in spending, especially military spending. To convince China that our economy was strong would require a herculean effort by the negotiating team that ignored certain realities. I maintained my silence; this was my first time flying on Air Force One, and I was a little starstruck. I would refrain from commenting until I felt I was on a surer footing or the president directly questioned me.

The next agenda point was to discuss Chinese commerce as it related to our trade deficit. The president wanted to persuade China to buy more US products. In the past, the United States was the largest market on earth. The Chinese had needed access to our buying power more than we had needed them. Times had changed, and the People's Republic of China now had the largest economy. The world was much more open to trade. If we did not buy Chinese products, they would sell them to someone else. We needed them more than they needed us. This weakness was not only with China. In the past, the Middle East sold most of its oil to the US. If we produced more oil or purchased from other regions like Venezuela, the Arab nations would suffer. That was no longer true. If we slowed our oil purchases, they would sell their oil to other energy-hungry countries—like China. America's economic power when it came to energy resources and products was weak and getting weaker.

The final agenda item was for China to support and protect US intellectual property rights. Western countries widely believed that China was stealing intellectual property. The Chinese government had been pleading ignorance for decades. No administration had been able to gain support from the Chinese, let alone have them admit to the transgressions. I believed all three agenda items were on shaky ground. I had little hope the leadership of the world's largest economy would see fit to placate our needs.

Upon arriving in Beijing, the president of China welcomed the US president and his entourage in grand fashion. There was a military parade—I suspect more to intimidate the US president with a show of power than to impress him. There was a social gathering to meet the upper echelon of the Chinese leadership. Then the US envoys were allowed time in their luxurious accommodations to prepare for the state dinner. The dinner was more lavish than usual for the US representatives. The pomp and circumstance were magical. There were Chinese dancers and Jiuniang (Chinese rice wine) to lighten the mood. Although our hosts told us what we were eating, most of us could not pronounce most of the dishes even when we had just heard the names. I got Tripe Soup and Stinky Tofu right. I did better than most. Dessert was an exceptional Chocolate Chinese Five-Spice Cake, with a fortune cookie—although I think the cookie was to poke fun at the Americans. Dessert came with Yunnan Coffee.

The next day, negotiations began. The plan was to have a day where the staffs coordinated the agenda and discussed etiquette and customs. There was tension in the meeting as the Chinese representatives seemed concerned when the Americans brought up their agenda items. Both sides wanted to talk about trade policy but from different angles. Financial issues also seemed quizzical to the Chinese staff. The Chinese believed they were overly generous to America, yet the Americans came to Beijing to ask for more. The coordination finished, but there was no coherent feeling that the negotiations with the two presidents would be cordial or result in progress between the new nations.

When the staff briefed the US president on the coordination session, he was concerned. He and his senior staff privately worked out a strategy to ease the Chinese president's concerns and curry favor for US issues. After the meeting, the US president felt prepared to represent America's needs.

The meeting began with a discussion of US bonds. The Chinese president said his nation had no plans to change its investment strategy regarding the United States. However, based on the current level of debt and the US government's unwillingness to control future spending, the Chinese president said he expected that the interest rates on US bonds would continue to increase to compensate for the risks. Although our president was concerned about rising interest rates, the fact was that for now, China would help fund US government spending. It was a relief to the president.

The mood shifted when the US president began talking about trade. He wanted the Chinese markets to be open to more US companies. China's president wanted the US to cancel all tariffs on Chinese exports to the US. Both presidents tried to relay the specific nuances of their positions, but neither was successful at changing the other's position. Thus, there was no improvement on trade.

The US president was concerned about the lack of progress thus far in the negotiations. Now he had to breach the most sensitive of the planned agenda items; intellectual property. For years the US claimed Chinese companies lured American industry to set up factories in China with enticements of cheap labor and access to their consumer market of approximately 1.7 billion people. Once the American company set up shop in China, a Chinese factory would open and produce the same product. Based on the Chinese president's reaction and my experience with the Chinese people, I could tell this accusation was an afront. The mood of the meeting went from mildly uncomfortable to adversarial. The Chinese president stated he would always put the best interest of China's people ahead of any other foreign country. He further expressed his displeasure with the inference that China was a less than honorable country and unable to compete with America without deception. The meeting adjourned with formal pleasantries but little attempts at true congeniality.

As I was in my suite preparing to leave China, I reviewed the day's activities. The US president had not needed me there; I did not influence the discussion. China's president out-maneuvered him. In fairness, the US president did not have much with which to bargain. Over the years, the US had depleted its leverage with other countries. We were no longer the largest economy. The US dollar was weak, and the yuan had become the world's reserve currency. Our military was more vulnerable, and we had begun reducing our worldwide policing efforts. The demoralized US president would have to come to terms with the realization that the US would have to use real diplomacy and could not buy or muscle support.

Everybody on the flight home ignored me. The president and all of his Democratic staff no longer had a use for me. I knew this was the only time I would fly on Air Force One until a Republican won the presidency, so I enjoyed the ride.

* * *

THE FORMER VICE president's inauguration as the new president of the United States of America occurred on January 20, 2037. It was a beautiful day in Washington, and the crowd size reflected it. The estimate was that over 900,000 people attended the inauguration event. That was not a surprise, as his predecessor was very popular and enthusiasm carried forward. Though the crowd did not match the numbers of former President Obama, it was quite impressive. Of course, some Republicans said Donald Trump's crowds were bigger yet.

The Democrats maintained all their members in the House during the presidential election year and picked up two previously held Republican seats from Oklahoma and North Dakota. The liberals in the House of Representatives made their majority 270 to 165. At the same time, Senate Democrats picked up one seat by replacing a retiring senator from Alaska to push their lead from 61 to 41. Washington would remain a one-party town.

After years of neglect, the Port of New York could no longer ignore its degrading infrastructure. Its seaports and airports needed massive renovations. The city floated a $130 billion bond to cover the costs. Because many of the port's responsibilities were joint efforts with New Jersey, that state also floated a $50 billion bond for renovations. The bulk of the funding again came from China. Once the money was there, massive projects began. The Red Hook and GCT Bayonne Container Terminal had reached their capacity. The port focused on re-engineering the areas to increase capacity and modernize transferring machinery. The project lasted three years and cost $46 billion. Modernization of the port's cruise ship terminals followed. The Brooklyn Cruise Terminal, GCT New York Terminal, and Cape Liberty Cruise Port were outdated, and cruise ship operators were diverting their business to more modern ports. These modifications were part of the upgrade as the container terminal changes neared completion. The cost to renew the cruise terminals was $34 billion.

New Jersey began upgrades to their Port Newark Container Terminal, Maher Terminal, and APM Terminals. Most of the remainder of New York's funds went to replacing aging runways and upgrading airport terminals. New Jersey contributed to repairs for Newark Liberty International. John F. Kennedy International Airport, Newark Liberty International Airport, and LaGuardia Airport consumed about $39 billion of New York's money. The remaining billion went to the feeder and general aviation airports throughout the region. These renovations were said to keep the New York area ports marketable for the next 25 years.

The federal government's legislators again targeted the military for spending cuts. After heated discussions on the floor of both the House of Representatives and the Senate, leadership decided that a joint committee would evaluate the depth of needed cuts. The committee's results would be binding.

Cuts were needed. Although China had agreed to continue funding US bonds, the pool of countries willing to take the risk was shrinking. The Chinese were also correct that the interest rates on those bonds would rise. After the last inflation numbers, it was time for the government to address the changes and increase interest rates.

While the committee on the military budget was meeting behind closed doors, politicians from all levels of the federalist system were lobbying to keep their bases open. They also fought to keep the manufacturers that produced military goods in their district from being affected. These efforts were not just in the halls of congress; the mainstream media and social media played a part in getting citizens involved and encouraged them to contact their elected officials for support.

When the committee published its report, a 20 percent cut to current military spending was needed to move toward sustainable budgets. The committee warned that similar future reductions in military expenditures would again occur. They also recommended significant reductions in discretionary spending and a review of current entitlements. Entitlements were always a very dangerous topic in Washington. Few politicians can broach the topic of cutting welfare, Social Security, and Medicare without losing their seats in the Congress, Senate, or the White House. Those debates usually incite rioting in the offending legislator's district and re-call efforts launched if the voters are unwilling to wait for the next election.

The Joint Chiefs of Staff (JCS) Chairman said the cuts were draconian and would devastate our military's ability to complete the tasks the president and Congress assigned them. The JCS also stated readiness to defend the country against current threats would be severely hampered. Our active duty and reserve forces needed to be ready to fight large-scale conflicts with China or Russia. At the same time, new cyber threats were increasing exponentially. The defense of those threats was very costly. With their concerns ignored and the cuts implemented, the chairman and two other joint chiefs resigned.

Legislators and military leaders began fighting for their priorities. The generals wanted to maintain troop strength and military equipment procurement programs, and the legislators wanted to reduce the impact of their cuts to their districts. Many in Congress claimed they would never support a committee that had binding powers again. Some began proceedings to undo the latest dictates, but they were unsuccessful.

In the end, the cuts occurred, and military readiness became severely depleted. The military stopped recruiting, and they eliminated re-enlistments for most career fields. They had stop-loss measures for critical areas, but it was all hard on morale. Many of the essential skills of military personnel were also very sought-after skills in the private market. By preventing those troops from leaving the service when they completed their enlistment, the military drastically reduced a soldier's future civilian career progression and income.

Military service members were receiving less training. Annual recurrent training changed to every other year. Schools that remained open shortened their syllabi and graduated those students in short order. Many of the smaller military bases closed, while the large bases had massive reductions in numbers. Legislators were happy if they still had a base in their district. There were additional cuts in the number of international bases. In South Korea, where the United States maintained over 26 instillations, 20 closed. That was a considerable reduction in military and financial support to our most important ally in the region. North Korea had not been friendly to the US in the 70 years since the Korean conflict, so they were pleased with the current developments.

Several high-profile weapon systems also met the budget ax. The military had a hard time defending some of those programs. After the expensive B-2 bomber that cost $500 million a copy and dropped few bombs on our adversaries in its lifetime, many in Congress were very suspicious of large programs and frequently mistrusted the military's rationalization for procurements. Most of the larger projects were reduced in scope, while smaller ventures faced outright elimination.

After all the cuts, our military was weaker. The only legislators who saved their jobs were those with the most seniority and salesmanship skills. Many junior members of Congress and senators lost their seats as voters retaliated against the loss of jobs and economic growth.

The president was a student of history and an insatiable reader. After we returned from China, the president talked to his chief of staff and opined that societies and their governments had lifespans. Americans assumed we would be the dominant form of government in the world forever, but there were weaknesses in that theory. The US dollar was no longer the leading currency in the world. That change flooded the world market with US dollars, causing inflation and weakening US economic power in the marketplace. China's economy surpassed ours, again reducing our dominance in the world market. Other countries courted China for access to their 1.7 billion customers. In the future, the US would need to be more accommodating to other countries and would have to woo them rather than bully them.

For now, the president felt compelled to ensure Americans felt safe in their beliefs. He tasked his staff to pen a statement that framed the China visit as a success for America. The fear was that it would highlight our fiscal irresponsibility by stressing China's willingness to continue funding our debt. They talked up progress in trade and intellectual property protection. They very carefully crafted the words to ensure the president was not lying, but the true nature of the Chinese president's responses was absent.

During the rainy season in South America, there was a landslide just outside Quito, Ecuador. The city's population was 1.8 million. The initial death toll was difficult to estimate. Much of the area consisted of make-shift homes with several generations of families living together. Geologists estimated 17,000 pounds of rocks moved. The US sent $2 billion in aid that included water, food, and medicine to help the stricken area. Additionally, 3,000 soldiers went there to help search for survivors and recover the victims. The president ordered the USS Mercy to help the region care for the injured. Unfortunately, by the time the ship arrived, there was not much need for the hospital beds. They transitioned as much space as they could to a morgue.

California was in financial trouble. The wildfire season was hard on California, and the state's other problems impacted resources before the fires. State and major metropolitan areas had been trying for 20 years to reduce their homeless population. Many of the proposed solutions had been costly with few positive results. Additionally, many major corporations had left the state. Their chief complaint was high taxes. With businesses leaving, many well-paying jobs departed also. Some legislators had made good faith efforts to reconcile the budget to control out-of-control spending. Unfortunately, because Californians had little tolerance for cutting services or benefits, tax increases on the wealthy were the only palatable course of action to the population. Those increases fell heavily on businesses, large and small. There came the point where the state government was unable to make payments on their debt and chose to default on the

2027 $800 billion infrastructure bond issue. The Chinese were the largest owners of the bonds. In this unusual event, they could negotiate with the bond trustee to take minority ownership of several seaports and airports instead of losing everything. The state was receptive because it wanted to keep China as an investor for future bond issues. If China lost its entire investment, it would be less likely to buy California's bonds in the future. Based on US economics, it was possible that additional funding would be needed.

The US Stock market was highly volatile in 2037. High inflation the previous year had spooked many investors. For the year, the Dow Jones Industrial Average lost nearly 15 percent of its value with unnerving swings. The chairman of the Federal Reserve took steps to dampen the fluctuations, but by the end of the year, he had little success.

The federal debt at the end of 2036 was $117 trillion, with a budget to ensure another $10 trillion scheduled for 2037. Considering the size of the deficit, the trivial increase in revenue was inconsequential. Total receipts for the year were $6.5 trillion. The total debt at the end of 2037 was $128 trillion.

2038

MY POPULARITY IN Texas continued to grow as jobs with good pay and benefits continued to migrate from high tax states like California, Illinois, and New York. Although I had little to do with the influx, I accepted most of the credit for the growth as a maturing politician. There were academic studies into the migration and its side effects. Although the financial benefit to the region included significant construction, large housing projects, and bulging tax coffers, the Republicans saw a considerable weakening in their legislative stronghold in the state. The result of people moving from high tax states and voting in Texas for the same things that hurt their old states was proving troublesome.

Those liberal policies increased spending beyond revenue, causing debt to rise inevitably. These activist politicians increased regulations which increased the cost to business and reduced personal liberties. Once established, these taxes and policies continued regardless of which party gained power in the future. Although Republicans might want to reduce those programs, it is challenging to remove the program without political fallout once the public receives a benefit. That fallout might mean a Republican would lose their seat to a Democrat who would re-establish and increase the spending.

This trend was hard to slow. The Democrats had a much easier product to sell. They promised benefits that were free or at least paid for by someone else, usually the allusive ill-defined "rich." Even when they defined the rich, the math usually showed that a sectors' increased tax would not supply the revenue needed to cover a proposed program. That is assuming the rich do not take steps to avoid the tax, which they inevitably will. This was the beginning of turning Texas into a high tax state. Giving people benefits they had not earned was an attractive proposition since the consequences were too far in the future for the population to visualize.

The Republicans stressed self-reliance and small government with few benefits. All governments begin by producing few services. They might promise much more, but the beginning is austere. As the country grows, politicians who want to get elected keep promising more and more programs. There is never an end of programs to spend money on, but there are limited resources. Although governments can tax, at some point, the taxes are too high, and those that are paying them will leave. Although I could see the burgeoning problems gestating, the coffers were full for now, jobs were plentiful, and I was getting the credit. However, there was mounting pressure to establish policies that had hurt other states.

In Washington, DC, I was still having difficulty getting my legislation passed. I introduced a bill supporting gun owners. That bill never made it out of committee. I submitted another with the support of several powerful co-sponsors to reduce debt growth and slow the increase in overall debt. It, too, was voted down in committee. I worked with some Democratic senators on bills that did not conflict with my core beliefs. Once the final bill was complete, the language made the legislation unpalatable to me, and I had to remove my name as a co-sponsor. I could see the US Senate was just as divided as the House of Representatives, and getting any bi-partisan work accomplished would be impossible. Neither side would do what was best for the country, only what was best for their party or to retain their seat. It was frustrating.

We added a child to our family. We planned on it being the first of three. For now, a new child that was happy and healthy with ten fingers and ten toes was a blessing. We spent as much time as possible with our new addition and started planning for their future.

* * *

THE YEAR 2038 was challenging for metropolitan areas. In January, Los Angeles was the first city to file for bankruptcy. The event sent shockwaves throughout the country since this was the largest city to prove insolvent. Detroit had filed a couple of decades ago, due to the loss of the auto industry to China, South Korea, Mexico, and Europe as the manufacturers sought lower wages for their employees. The Los Angeles filing was not the result of one cataclysmic event but rather decades of overspending. Most analysts saw it coming years ahead of the actual date. The same was true later in the year when Seattle, San Francisco, and Chicago filed for bankruptcy.

Although the details varied by city, they had followed similar approaches in their efforts to maintain financial solvency through reduction of expenditures. The first cost saving was retiree pay. Over the years, many municipalities had promised public unions unrealistic defined benefit plans to garner political support. As the unions grew and the number of retirees climbed, the unfunded payment programs became more of a burden. In bankruptcy, Los Angeles reduced government employee retirement payments by 30 percent, causing outrage from current retirees and employees. This was only the beginning of the cost-saving measures. The city required those eligible to transition to Medicare and lose their Los Angeles paid medical coverage. It cost retirees hundreds of millions of dollars in increased medical expenses and prescription drug costs. The unions filed lawsuits but lost.

The city also reduced its number of current employees. The mayor tried to shield the police force as he believed it had the proper number of personnel. However, 10 percent of the force was let go from service. The same fate fell on the fire department—17 percent of the firefighters were gone. This resulted in delayed service for fires. Even the local school districts were affected. Los Angeles did not have direct control over school districts, but they could restrict city payments. The mayor reduced payments to the schools by 25 percent. City-run hospitals were cut by 20 percent, resulting in longer wait times at emergency rooms. Those that did get beds in ERs would have to wait a day or more for a bed in the hospital because of a lack of nurses. People also had to wait longer to get appointments with their primary care physician as well as specialists. Two out of three ambulances were in disrepair, creating long delays for paramedics to arrive. Surgeries were delayed or canceled. Finally, the department of public works received a 25 percent cut. As a result, power outages lasted longer, and the roads did not receive timely repairs. All utilities were negatively affected by the cuts. There were riots in the streets nightly. These were hard times for Los Angeles and those cities that followed it into bankruptcy.

It had not taken long before the effects of the cuts became apparent. Crime increased 400 percent. The lack of police emboldened the criminals, and the district attorney was unwilling to charge the arrested, resulting in the release of criminals. This frustrated the remaining police officers, so they stopped arresting people. Businesses faced looting, forcing many small shops to close permanently. Even some large stores closed their downtown Los Angeles properties to protect their employees and because of the increasing cost of security and repairs.

The city defaulted on many of its bonds, resulting in a cavalcade of lawsuits from creditors.

Because the courts were severely understaffed, it took months to get a hearing.

Los Angeles still needed operating funds. They began liquidating tangible assets. City parks were the first to go. Knowing the city's dire straits, investors were willing to pay far below market rates for the land. When the city tried to attach riders to the sale, the price dropped further. The city was afraid the parks would turn into apartments or retail establishments, which they were. Therefore, they required the land remain a park for ten years after the sale. Investors pulled their bids until the city managers removed the condition. The city also owned 25 percent of the art displayed in museums and city buildings. Again, city management wanted to attach a rider allowing Los Angeles to buy back the art within ten years at the price they sold it. In essence, the city was asking for an interest-free loan, with the art as collateral. Buyers again balked, and the city managers relented.

The Los Angeles transit system shut down. The rail system became unsafe because of a lack of maintenance, and the city could no longer afford the liability. The bus system halted as slow maintenance caused more vehicles to be unserviceable, and paying the drivers for not driving was unsustainable. These shutdowns hurt the poor most of all, and there were many more poor people every day. The unemployed teachers, police, firefighters, civil engineers, and librarians all filled the social welfare offices to do what they could to put food on their table, stressing the city, county, state, and local governments' budgets enormously. It took weeks for the social services offices to process the claims, delaying the needed relief.

The same fate was prevalent in Seattle, San Francisco, and Chicago. Although the details and percentages varied, the pain was widespread, and the shockwaves extended well beyond their city limits. The crumbling of a major city caused reduced tax revenue for county and state coffers as well.

After years of increased importance, the Chinese yuan became the global currency, marking 20 years of decline in the US dollar's impact and China's strong economy. It was a concerted effort by China to usurp the US currency. Countries around the world had held dollars in reserve. In recent years, they maintained a balance of dollars and yuan as a hedge. Now that China had won the battle, those countries began dumping their US currency.

The flood of US dollars in the market caused staggering inflation of 53 percent. This dramatic increase in the cost of living had an astonishing effect on most Americans. The poor ended up becoming more impoverished, and many more people had to apply for government assistance to survive. Small businesses had to change their business model to include fewer employees and demand more of those that remained. As unemployment climbed, the number of people receiving unemployment benefits and welfare checks rose. There were more needy people, and the government payments did not keep up with inflation. Crime increased in all cities and most towns across America. Americans were hurting, and the government had taken away their ability to help themselves.

During the last ten years, stock market growth had been anemic and slowed to only 1 percent in 2037. This year, the stock market (Dow Jones Industrial Average) took a 7,000-point hit, dropping from a high of 46,525 to 39,175. The impact on retirement accounts was devastating. People who had jobs but wanted to retire had to continue working if they could, meaning fewer opportunities for those who hoped to fill their vacated positions. Worker's 401K/IRA programs lost 20 to 30 percent of their values, encouraging investors to take additional risks to regain their losses. Most of those risks were foolhardy and ended with more severe reductions in their retirement fund's value.

Fewer foreign countries continued to fund America's debt. China stayed true to its word and bought more US treasuries as they became available, but at much higher interest rates. At 12 percent interest, the US government needed more money just to service the existing debt.

Another hurricane season had arrived, and the first tropical storm was approaching America's southeastern region. This time FEMA was slow to respond due to budget cuts and changing priorities within the government. When Hurricane Allen made landfall 40 miles north of Fort Lauderdale, it was a category two storm with winds topping out at 105 miles per hour. Although it was not a catastrophic storm, FEMA and other emergency services' failure to act early amplified the damage and the aftermath. The result was $65 billion in unbudgeted damages.

The federal debt at the end of 2037 was $128 trillion. The budget ensured another $11.5 trillion scheduled for 2038 without considering any natural disasters. The country had $6.7 trillion in revenue, but the Gross Domestic Product showed signs of weakness. If the GDP began to fall, it was reasonable to expect revenues to follow suit. The total debt at the end of 2038 was $141 trillion.

2039

I FOUND GREAT joy in spending time with my growing family. Our young daughter was growing quickly, and we were preparing for our second child. However, my joy was short-lived. My father passed away from a heart attack. He was only 63 years old, and we were very close. We would fish and hunt as I was growing up. It was a great bonding time for us. We continued to get together for our outings after I moved out, but the hunting and fishing trips got further apart as I became busier with my life. I regret not making more effort to spend time with him. He was a brilliant man and an inspiration to me throughout my life. I would miss him terribly.

My father had grown up in San Francisco and wanted his burial to be in the family plot. I took my family and my mother to California. Although my mother was the executor of the will, I took care of most of the details and only bothered her for signatures. Although it was good to see family, the reason for the gathering was regrettable. It was a somber event that I will never forget.

Back in Texas, I threw myself into work. To get a better understanding of my state's energy infrastructure, I visited Texas energy centers. The petrochemical industry center was in Houston and Midland/Odessa. I met with several chief executive officers and chief operating officers to understand their operations and how the government could help them. Those companies accounted for hundreds of millions in tax revenue annually, and supporting them was in the best interest of Texas. The Electric Reliability Council of Texas (ERCOT) controls most of the state's energy (approximately 75 percent), except for the oil in the eastern counties.

My next stop was in northcentral Texas, where the bulk of Texas' windmill farms were. Due to legislation in the early 2000s, Texas required the transition to renewable energy. Texas gets a higher percentage of energy from the wind (nearly 30 percent) than most states. Although wind energy is costly compared to petroleum products, it is very popular. The hope was that the price would continue to drop as the technology matured. The common theme from the executives in both oil and wind was for the government to be less intrusive. Although the executives enjoyed the subsidies, they did not want the oversight and regulations that accompanied them.

* * *

THE YEAR BEGAN with a government stand-off with a white supremacist group holding 13 hostages, mostly women and children. They had blockaded themselves in a ranch outside of Cimarron, New Mexico, with rations, considerable arms, and ammunition. The primary house was stone, the outer buildings of wood. The home was two stories with a basement, and the second floor had good vantage points for protecting the home. They demanded the resignation of the president of the United States, the New Mexico governor, and much of the state legislature. The FBI was in charge of defusing the situation and estimated 15 to 20 white supremacists were inside. After a 33-day stand-off, a plausible solution still did not exist. Public interest had waned weeks ago. On February 2, the FBI breached the northwest side of the compound. Gunfire immediately erupted. When the smoke cleared, four white supremacists were in custody, with thirteen dead. All of the hostages died; four men, three women, and six children, all shot in the head.

The media ran with the story. They sharply criticized the FBI's handling of the situation. The FBI director defended the actions of her agents and admitted she was involved in the decision to breach the compound. She was trying to shield the commander-in-chief from blame as the presidential campaign was beginning. There were major issues the president was confronting, and the New Mexico domestic terrorist situation needed defusing.

The election season was in full swing early in the year. Billions of dollars were spent nationwide. The Republicans fought hard to get their message out that runaway spending had to stop. Our financial status crippled our ability to grow and be the generous nation we had always been.

In recent history, the Democrats had been adding to their majorities in off-year elections. The Democratic National Committee (DNC) pushed hard to keep that trend going. They spent billions of dollars nationwide on mainstream media buys. They also optimized social media outlets to reach the younger demographics. The Republican National Committee was keenly aware of the current disparity in Congress and outspent the DNC by four percent. This year, the RNC

made significant inroads with social media plat-
forms to help their candidates. The RNC and DNC
funds combined with the individual candidates'
spending made this the most expensive mid-term
election in history. When the voting ended, the
Democrats picked up five House seats, two from
retiring congress members. The Republicans won
five additional seats, four from retiring Democrats.
The end result was the make-up of the House of
Representatives remained the same, with 270
Democrats and 165 Republicans. The media outlets
were thrilled with the money spent, but America
was no better or worse off.

Because of the increased US debt and staggering inflation, the interest rates on bonds increased
to 13.7 percent. The result increased the interest in other financial instruments such as home
mortgages, credit cards, and business loans. As
the cost of borrowing money increased, fewer
people took out those loans to expand their businesses, further slowing economic growth and
reducing GDP. Economists believed tax revenue
was a reflection of GDP, although not a direct
correlation. Generally, when GDP falls, tax revenues decrease as well. Historically, tax revenue in
the US was approximately 20 percent of GDP. If
there was a ten percent reduction in GDP, then tax
collection would fall a similar amount. With the
steady increase in federal spending, a reduction

in revenue would result in a disproportionate increase in our deficit.

There was another string of municipal bankruptcies in 2039. It started with Detroit filing again, combined with Pittsburgh, Atlanta, and Denver. Because Detroit was insolvent before, they had fewer options for recovery. Although many of their personnel reductions had recovered to pre-bankruptcy levels, they had terminated the retirement programs and reduced many benefit packages. The other cities took those cost-cutting measures now, but Detroit had to cut its employees significantly deeper than the other cities. The unrest that followed resulted in lawsuits in the more genteel groups, but rioting and looting were far more prevalent. These actions resulted in businesses closing or relocating to less volatile areas outside of the city. The recovery for Detroit took a long time. Their roads, bridges, sewer, and water systems were older and needed more maintenance than the other cities. Detroit had higher unemployment and welfare rolls prior to the bankruptcy than the other cities. The public unrest and destruction in Detroit were horrific.

Although the previous two years had been hard on municipalities, this year brought corporate failures to the forefront. Major corporations filed for bankruptcy because their management lost focus on profits and became too political. The

Walt Disney Company had to divest itself of ESPN and Marvel and cut its pace of movie output in half as revenue plummeted. Disney also closed most of its international parks to focus on California and Florida as attendance did not keep up with costs.

General Electric sold their aviation and health care departments. They held onto their renewable energy division—although the operations were losing money, the massive government subsidies made them worth keeping. The future of those subsidies was uncertain. Although national politicians wanted to continue subsidizing green energy, the plight of the federal budget made those investments less assured. That scenario played out in corporate board rooms across America. Many sought new investments to remain solvent, with some foreign countries providing the influx of money in exchange for equity shares in major US companies. Some of those countries took a controlling interest in formerly US corporations.

The Dow Jones Industrial Average continued its decline, dropping 11,000 points to 28,348, dealing a death blow to many people's retirement accounts. The decline pressured many elderly people who were physically able to return to the workforce. However, they discovered there were few opportunities for those who did not have current marketable skills. Even if the retirees had worked in the tech industries, they had been out of the market too long, and their skills were of little current value. Those who were nearing retirement were remaining on the job longer in hopes of their 401K recovering. When you combined the fall in the value of retirement savings and the reduced buying power due to inflation, retirement was now out of reach for most Americans.

With this year's fall in the market values combined with last year, the US Gross Domestic Product had decreased by 40 percent, further reducing income to federal coffers.

The US continued closing military bases. Small bases worldwide had already been shut in previous cost-cutting efforts. Their services transferred to larger facilities. Now the larger bases had a target on them. To reduce the number of lost votes for weakened economic activity due to base closures, Congress initially focused on foreign bases. These foreign base closures were concerning to our allies. There was also a cost to US readiness. Many of these foreign bases stored equipment in the event of conflicts in those regions. Without the forward bases' supplies, our reaction time to a potential war was longer than it used to be. The US shifted its military doctrine from policing the world to becoming more entrenched to protect our homeland, shortening our reach, and reducing the cost of maintaining our supply chains. Unfortunately, the closure of foreign bases was inadequate. Major

US bases also became targets for closure. Leadership established priorities for programs and services to keep. The Pentagon complained about the reduction in the readiness of our forces, but its concerns fell on deaf ears.

As US forces returned home, many personnel got their release from service to their country. To those that were career-minded soldiers, they had to change their aspirations quickly. Regardless of the soldiers' career intentions, those let go found a difficult job market. Most military service jobs do not lend themselves to civilian skills. Historically, soldiers, sailors, and airmen disproportionately moved from military jobs to other government-related employment. They would become police officers, firefighters, or other civil service employees. With the current flood of applicants, there were few of those jobs available.

The US reduction in force size and reach gave China an opening. The Chinese strategically filled the void left by US military departures in Europe, the Pacific, Africa, and Asia. Military leadership saw this force proliferation as an ominous move by the Chinese.

American cities continued to deal with underfunded infrastructure. Rolling blackouts plagued many major cities, from New York to Seattle, throughout the summer. The loss of electricity during the hot months caused air conditioning units to fail, hurting the elderly and infirm the most. Hospitals were also affected. They had generators to supply critical functions, but working conditions were difficult. The blackouts caused car accidents as traffic light operations were intermittent. Overall, hundreds of people died across the country due to infrastructure failures, and millions became inconvenienced.

The blackouts also increased crime in most metropolitan areas. With inflation reaching 31 percent, companies were reducing staff as revenues dropped, increasing unemployment and homelessness. With the despair came more looting. Those that were unemployed applied for public assistance, but the benefits were not keeping up with prices. Some made do with less; the rest resorted to crime. With rolling blackouts, security systems didn't work. Because of the increase in crime, the police response was slow. These factors gave criminals a sense of invulnerability and, therefore, emboldened them.

As America's need for investments continued to increase, the country sold more bonds. China continued to buy most of the issuances—at ever-increasing interest rates.

Under cost-cutting ideas, Congress began debating whether the money given to the World Health Organization (WHO) was money well spent. The US provided the WHO with approximately

$600 million or over 20 percent of its total budget. Democrats believed the WHO provided the most impoverished nations health care and preventative care. Republicans believed the money went to an anti-American organization and that today the US needed the money to provide health and preventive care to Americans.

In the past four years, inflation averaged 19.5 percent. The cumulative effect over the last fifteen years had devastated the buying power of the American consumer. Retiree savings were overwhelmed by the reduction in the buying power of their savings, requiring increased government assistance when the U.S. and state governments could not afford to increase social security or welfare payments. Many elderly Americans who were living on their retirement income found themselves destitute. Some resorted to begging in the street, and it became reminiscent of the Great Depression.

Twenty years previously, the Government Accountability Office (GAO) estimated revenue from all sources in 2039 would put $6.83 trillion into the US Treasury, but the actual number was $3.6 trillion. It was a financial shortfall that politicians were unwilling to address through the legislative process. The result was more debt.

The federal debt at the end of 2038 was $141 trillion, with a budget to ensure another $11.2

trillion scheduled for 2039. The total debt at the end of 2039 was $155 trillion.

2040

THE STRESS OF being a parent and life in Washington DC caused tension in my family. Living in Washington was not the real problem; it was being a senator. The draw on my time was monumental. I attended social events a couple of times a week. We fought a lot, and I frequently went to official events alone. We were in love, but we wanted our kids to have two parents. It was affecting my work. I voted on bills I hadn't read, and I agreed to co-sponsor legislation I had not adequately researched. We decided counseling was the best move for our family. There were several therapists in the area that dealt with high-ranking government officials.

After we researched a few of them, I contacted our choice and made an appointment. We went to counseling once a week to start. My in-laws moved from San Francisco to Dallas to help take care of our children. They were a big help and relieved a lot of the stress in our home.

It was a presidential election year. I spent whatever time I could spare trying to get the Republican candidate elected without disrupting my marriage. I gave speeches to civic organizations and interviews on syndicated radio shows. Whatever television spots I could arrange, I participated in, even if it was on a liberal-leaning station. It had been a long time since the United States of America had a Republican president. I was hopeful.

* * *

THE DEMOCRATIC PRESIDENT was running for re-election. He was confident of his chances. At the beginning of his campaign, he was 23-points ahead of an as-of-yet unnamed opponent. After the Republicans picked the popular former governor from Georgia, the race tightened. The sitting president still had an 11-point lead as their campaigns gained traction. As with other recent elections, it was very contentious. Both sides exaggerated the claims against their opponent. The sitting president had more opportunity to push legislation to court votes than an ex-governor. He used that ability to his benefit and won re-election easily.

After the election, to address the unrest in the cities, Senate Democrats put forward a far-reaching gun law that would limit the number of guns an individual could own on a weighted scale. A handgun with more than seven rounds limited the number of pistols one could own. High-capacity rifles limited the number of rifles a person could have. The number of bullets purchased per month was also limited. The NRA poured millions of dollars into fighting the initiative. I fought the legislation hard and was successful along with other Republicans and some NRA Democrats at softening the bill, but in the end, we lost. The president signed the bill into law. The NRA sued, and many of the provisions were unconstitutional, yet gun owners were still limited.

Municipal bankruptcies continued in 2040. The biggest was New York City. Like the cities before, it cut pensions to city retirees and reduced their medical coverage. For those eligible for Medicare, they had to switch from the city's plan. To emerge from bankruptcy, the city cut employees by an average of 25 percent. The mayor focused on minimizing the losses to first responders, which meant he reduced other agencies disproportionately. Several departments were closed entirely - the Department for the Aging, the Department of Cultural

Affairs, and the Transitional Finance Authority. These cuts saved on salary, benefits, retirement, and overhead. The New York City Transit merged with the New York City Department of Transportation. Not all employees made the change to the new department. Due to redundancies, some jobs became obsolete. Other departments took significant budget cuts. The Board of Education budget took a 40 percent cut, while the Mayor's Office of Special Projects received a 60 percent decrease. Bus and train routes reduced their service by 25 percent overall. Philadelphia and Boston also filed for insolvency and suffered a similar plight as New York.

The rolling blackouts that had plagued the country the previous summer intensified in 2040. The costs of fixing the infrastructure were beyond the capabilities of the municipalities and the special districts that were responsible for them. For decades, citizens demanded cheap energy, and politicians obliged them. The energy districts had not been pricing their product correctly to account for long-term maintenance. Now that the bill was due, consequences were mounting.

In rural Oklahoma, just outside Dill City, a group of right-wing radicals held up in an old farmhouse. This was more problematic because there was a disproportionate number of women and children. The group leaders claimed to be a religious sect that believed in natural medicine and rejected doctors. They also rejected the sovereignty of the United States of America over their people. Failure to file taxes for the past 12 years led to their discovery. After repeated attempts by the Internal Revenue Service (IRS) to contact the farm's owner, agents went to the property. When they arrived, the people in the farmhouse produced guns and told them to leave their property. Using sound judgment, the IRS agents left and called the Federal Marshal in Oklahoma City.

A couple of miles away in Burns Flat was an old Strategic Air Command heavy bomber airfield. It was now the Clinton-Sherman Industrial Park in Washita County. This was fortuitous for the Marshal Service. They sent their initial reaction team there and the military used the airfield to reinforce the marshals. There was a stand-off reminiscent of the Waco siege of 1993. Government officials were keen to prevent a similar result where 76 people died inside the ranch, including 25 children and two pregnant women.

After some research, the ATF discovered an excellent probability of many high-capacity weapons at the Oklahoma farm. After three weeks of negotiations and substantial news coverage, the sect's leader sent all of his members out and then killed himself. Authorities found a large stockpile of weapons and ammunition, but thankfully, the leader lost his nerve and ended the stand-off.

Just three weeks later, there was a major earthquake in southern California. The quake was centered northeast of San Diego along the San Jacinto fault with an intensity measuring 7.6 on the Richter Magnitude Scale. There was considerable damage to buildings and roads within 20 miles of the epicenter. In San Diego, most significant buildings were unscathed due to building codes in California that required structures to withstand moderate earthquake events. Even so, the damages to the region exceeded $1.3 billion.

There was little latitude in the federal budget. Just over 35 percent of all revenue went to service the debt. Mandatory entitlement expenses claimed the next 47 percent, including Social Security, Medicare, Medicaid, and unemployment compensation. That left only 18 percent as discretionary spending. Of the discretionary spending, the vast majority was used for the military, leaving just under $700 billion to run all other facets of the US government.

The Dow Jones Industrial Average dropped 12,000 points to 16,789. This correlated to a 34 percent drop in GDP and a painful reduction in tax revenue to the US government. As the financial markets dropped, jobs were lost, increasing the need for government services, welfare, and unemployment.

Inflation increased again in 2040 to 44 percent. Washington legislators were still unwilling to take the necessary steps to curb the tide of excessive spending. The Federal Reserve raised interest rates to control the supply of money and bring down inflation. Inflation was the worst tax of all because it severely damaged the buying power and de-incentivized saving money for the future. If the inflationary period ended, there would be little savings, which would extend the consequences of the period.

The president, in a nationally televised address, claimed the US economy was officially in a depression. The economy had been shrinking for more than two years, and the GDP had dropped much more than 10 percent. Although people in financial sectors were well aware of the economic realities, politicians were reluctant to admit the dire situation until they couldn't avoid it any longer. After evading the issue for years, politicians had to face the fact that austerity measures would be needed. With the writing on the wall for the past 50 years, politicians would not face the fact that the continued spending could not last in perpetuity. Kicking the can to the next Congress was no longer an option.

The US financial crisis was worsening. The federal government began freezing foreign assets and US bank funds to stabilize the markets. Banks were buying up assets, while the Federal Reserve questioned whether these banks would ever be able to sell those assets back into the market.

Projected revenue from the GAO for 2040 was $7 trillion. In reality, receipts came in at just $2.53 trillion. The politicians that previously were clamoring to be on television were now avoiding the camera.

The federal debt at the end of 2039 was $155 trillion. With a budget to ensure another $12.6 trillion scheduled for 2040, the total debt at the end of 2040 was $171 trillion.

2041

I BATTLED WITH green energy. I know there is a limited supply of oil in the ground, and since the US made fracking illegal, we were becoming more dependent on foreign oil. The world's consumption of oil was accelerating and making that commodity even more scarce. To get America back to energy independence required alternatives. Republicans were against increased funding of wind and solar because they were too expensive and unreliable. Though I was considering supporting the financing of green energy, the deficit made that impractical. I was conflicted between smaller government and energy sources. There was not an easy answer.

We took the opportunity to use my in-laws for babysitting and went to Vermont for a skiing weekend. Although we averted injury, we had sore muscles on Monday that had us hobbling for days. We vowed to be more active every day and to take more vigorous trips together.

In the Senate, the Republicans were pushing to reduce or eliminate funding for Planned Parenthood. They were renewing their concerns about abortion. I hate abortion but did not feel it was my job to interfere with the decisions of a young couple or young woman about the most personal decision they would ever make. Also, I wouldn't say I liked the idea of using public funds to pay for them. The problem was that not using public funds eliminated the option for the poor who might be least able to afford to have the child. I disagreed with my Republican colleagues on this issue. I also disagreed with the Democrats wanting to make abortion too easy. The Republicans used their ideas as talking points but knew the Democrats would not allow a vote on the floor. I remained silent on the issue; there was nothing to be gained by entering the fray.

I began preparing for my re-election campaign coming up in 2042, spending the beginning of the year fundraising and garnishing support from the party leadership. I was surprised by how easy it was to raise funds. Texans saw the wave of Democrats in the halls of Congress and increasing in state legislatures. Even in Texas, they wanted to do their part to keep the state conservative. They also saw the migration of people from California, New York, Illinois, and other high tax states as a threat. If the new residents voted in Texas as they did in their previous homes, trouble was a-brewing.

The party leadership was happy with my performance on my committees, especially with my work on the Finance, Budget, and Banking committees. They put their support behind my re-election, and their backing set the Republican election machine in motion for funding, organization, and media buys. This should be my easiest election so far.

$$* * *$$

THE YEAR STARTED with the Presidential inauguration. Because of the economic state of the union, it was a much more modest event. The fanfare was minimized to avoid appearing uncaring about the suffering across the nation.

As a budgetary measure, three major military bases shut down. Fort Riley in Kansas was the first to close, followed by Hill and Tinker Air Force Bases (AFB). These Air Force bases were in the major metropolitan areas of Salt Lake City and Oklahoma City. Those cities had powerful lobbies fighting hard to keep their bases open. Base closures had a substantial financial impact on the region. The senators and congress members from their areas had meetings and hearings about the closures and tried to pressure the Department of Defense to reconsider their decision. Local businesses and political leaders used their resources to influence decision-makers. Despite their efforts, the bases closed, units decommissioned, and jobs were gone forever. The Air Force mothballed many of their aircraft in the desert. The Army transferred what equipment they could and retired the remainder. These closures, combined with the overall economic situation, devastated their states' economies.

All foreign subsidies were under consideration. Past contributions to foreign countries had risen as high as $42 billion annually, with Iraq, Afghanistan, Israel, Egypt, and Jordan each receiving more than $1 billion. In 2041, the total budget for foreign aid was less than $500 million. Because of our massive debt, we began seeking assistance from other countries. No other country reached out to help. In all fairness, their economies were weak as well. They had spent decades riding on the successes of the United States and were unprepared to stand on their own.

Congress was trying to increase revenue as the GDP continued to fall. They raised taxes, first on the rich, and then the reality hit that all income levels would need to pay more. The top marginal bracket went up to 75 percent. The lowest was 27 percent. Those that could took steps to prevent paying the higher levels of taxation. Corporate taxes also went up, and deductions were reduced. Congress all but eliminated the research and development tax deduction for businesses. Conservatives in Congress complained that companies would stop funding research and reduce American competitiveness for decades after the current financial crisis. They lost. In the end, the percentage of GDP collected in tax receipts only rose to 23 percent from the historic 20 percent. It did not make a substantial impact on our increasing debt.

Programs for the needy were the next target. Food stamp funding decreased by 25 percent. Women, Infant, & Children (WIC) food supplements went down by 20 percent, and school breakfast programs faced the ax. School lunch payments only took a reduction of 10 percent. Congress tried to keep as many assistance programs as possible because the poor were the most affected, but all levels of government felt the budgetary hardship.

Public universities faced shortfalls in student enrollments, budget cuts from government sources, and plummeting endowment donations.

The colleges released all non-tenured faculty, and those that remained had to endure pay cuts. Tenured faculty members sued for breach of contract, and many won. Forced with paying their faculty, some universities closed campuses. The administrative staff was cut by 50 percent, and the janitorial and maintenance staff faced a 40 percent cut. Private universities followed suit, and all but the most elite schools felt the pain.

The United States began removing itself from multi-national agreements. We could no longer afford the generous contributions offered by previous administrations. They tried to abide by the withdrawal protocols, but some were too cumbersome and lengthy. The US needed relief from the obligations quickly. Our departure opened diplomatic opportunities for other countries to fill; some of them were our adversaries.

The 2040 Census results again showed a migration of people from the high tax states to lesser taxed regions. This change in demographics changed the make-up of the US legislature. The biggest losers were California, New York, Illinois, and Massachusetts. The states that gained seats were Texas, Florida, Oklahoma, and Montana.

With less funding available for police departments, crime increased dramatically. Mobs were running roughshod over large sections of most cities. Violent crime and looting were commonplace in many communities. Murder increased nationwide by 103 percent in the past year. There was little concern the police would intervene. Their pay was cut, their city councils had restricted their ability to apprehend criminals, and the court system was unwilling to prosecute offenders. The mobs ruled, and the police tried to stay out of their way. If they acted, the political leadership would not have their backs.

For several years, the US military budgets had taken draconian cuts. These reductions resulted in massive degradation of military readiness worldwide. The Joint Chiefs of Staff believed the cuts had gone too far and began to discuss their options. The chairman of the JCS was the first to use the phrase "coup d'état." The room fell silent.

Once the totality of the idea sank in, the Joint Chiefs realized that might very well be their best option. They began discussing which generals and units were vital to making the plan work.

Each chief reached out to the major command generals they trusted. They focused on the commanders in the Washington, DC area. For a coup to succeed, capturing the nation's leadership would be key, requiring overwhelming force in the nation's capital. Support across all senior leadership would prevent uncooperative forces from retaking the capital once the initial attack was successful.

After careful planning, the JCS choose July 4, 2041, as the date of the attack. The plan was to capture the president, vice president, speaker, Senate majority leader, and the Supreme Court. Then the rebels would install the chairman of the Joint Chiefs as the new commander in chief and president.

The initial attack began at 3:00 A.M. It was a simultaneous attack on the president in the White House, the vice president in his residence at the Naval Observatory, the speaker, majority leader, and all the Supreme Court justices at their homes in the Washington area. Things did not go well from the beginning. The secret service and capitol police got the president to the bunker before the marines could seize him.

The vice president was not as lucky as the president. He died in the crossfire at his home, along with four Secret Service agents and two Washington, DC police officers. A sitting vice president had never before been killed in the history of the United States.

The speaker of the House of Representatives and the Senate majority leader were both captured. Most of the Supreme Court justices were able to elude apprehension. The generals were able to imprison the chief justice and two of the associate justices.

From the White House bunker, the president was able to rally military and police resources from outside the region to stop the attack. Within 48 hours, the capital was back in the administration's control. The coup d'état leadership went to prison. The members of the JCS that spearheaded the attacks were later tried for treason and put to death. In all, 937 soldiers died, with an additional 1,845 hospitalized. A total of 1,423 police officers and secret service agents died defending our country. Although the coup d'état failed, military morale and readiness took a significant hit. The coup d'état shook civilian leadership's trust in the military resulting in additional security measures for our country's leadership.

In 2041, the stock market lost 3,700-points, dropping to 13,100. The GDP fell 19 percent, and revenue decreased 17 percent. Ten years ago, the GAO had predicted the treasury would receive $7.18 trillion in revenue. In reality, only $1.98 trillion came in, yet spending continued to climb.

The federal debt at the end of 2040 was $171 trillion. The total debt at the end of 2041 was $188 trillion.

2042

I WANTED MY campaign for re-election to focus on our continued excessive government spending, but the people of Texas were not concerned with that. They were concerned with jobs, inflation, retirement, and safety. Government spending was not a concern. They did not appreciate the gravity of the crushing public debt and the causal relationship to inflation, which was the underlying cause of America's woes. Many politicians lacked an understanding of economics and believed government could spend America back to prosperity. This was the battle I had to fight in my campaign, trying to fix the symptoms of the problem (jobs, inflation, retirement, and safety) rather than the true cause of the pain (government overspending). This was while the government's spending increased exponentially.

The president asked me to join a committee to study and address Chinese Human Rights violations. It was an attempt to appear bi-partisan by putting a Republican on a committee that was not important to voters. This had been a long-term issue; the Chinese had violated human rights since the 1930s. They had suppressed Muslims and went through a phase of only allowing one child per family. They also had been accused of child trafficking. Through the years, their violations had varied but continued. The US had tried to pressure Beijing to modify its policies, but again the US had little leverage to affect change.

My campaign was hard-fought, but my lead never went below eight points. There was a move across the nation against the established party, and that helped me. On election night, my family and I watched the election results from our apartment in Plano, Texas. When my opponent conceded, I moved to a nearby hotel ballroom where my supporters had gathered to celebrate.

* * *

THE TREASURY WAS ready to sell $18 trillion in US bonds to fund the authorized spending. The bonds had an interest rate of 14 percent—an increase from the previous year. Only 75 percent of the bonds issued found buyers. The US government could print money and cause our already high inflation to increase exponentially or make more draconian cuts in spending. They selected a combination of the two. Unfortunately, there was not time to methodically cut the budget. There was an order for a 15 percent cut across all agencies, combined with a two trillion influx of cash issued by the treasury to close the gap of the failed bond issue. As expected, those actions caused a two percent increase in interest rates, and inflation climbed to over 60 percent.

In preparation for future budget battles, Congress began marking programs for reduction or elimination. Government services and infrastructure continued to crumble. The government canceled WIC payments and reduced welfare payments as the buying power of the dollar was eroding. The military absorbed another 20 percent cut. Nearly all foreign bases closed. Those that remained open had minimal staff. Recruitments practically stopped, with only the most critical jobs filled. Because of the reduced benefits, there were not enough applicants to fill those slots. Most re-enlistments halted, and the government enacted an additional ten percent cut across all facets of federal operations. One brave Republican representative even had the temerity to suggest cutting congressional pay and pensions.

Regardless of America's financial situation, the weather did not change. A hurricane headed to Florida. Although aware of the situation, FEMA had few resources left to react to the pending storm. As the hurricane ravaged the east coast of Florida, floodwaters raised havoc on Miami, Fort Lauderdale, and surrounding communities. Critical services were slow to respond to the needs of those affected. There were significant costs attributed to the damages. Repairs were slow, and the region would take a decade to recover. There was simply no funding available to respond more quickly.

Crime increased nationwide. Gangs had become larger, more aggressive, and emboldened. Many municipalities had cut police pay, and when some were slow with paychecks, the blue flu sprang up and cops didn't show up for work.

The president of China died suddenly. He was 89 years old and in poor health. He was obese with the ailments associated with that condition. He had groomed his grandson to take over when he retired—his death expedited his grandson's ascent to the presidency.

Based on the new Chinese president's first public speech, our relationship would change. He expressed a more nationalist view than his grandfather. He promised more investments in China. He would allow less money to support foreign countries unless there was a direct correlation to benefit China. The new president voiced a more hardline communist direction for his country.

The Democrats suffered unexpected losses in the mid-term elections. Because of the state of our economy, the tide was turning against all incumbent politicians. State legislatures, governorships, and the federal legislature saw a wave of Republicans elected along with a few Independent candidates. Representation in the House of Representatives made a considerable change, but the Democrats still maintained control with 241 Democrats, 189 Republicans, and five Independents. In the Senate, Republicans gained five seats and changed the ratio to 56 Democrats to 46 Conservatives. The liberals still maintained control of the government, but by a smaller margin.

Foreign subsidies and charitable contributions became a thing of the past. The countries that relied on them to meet their budget had to find other ways to raise revenue. Some sought help from other countries. China and Russia were willing to help as the US receded.

Infrastructure was becoming a bigger problem. Several bridges in New York City had to be closed. The H-3 Tunnel in Honolulu was closed with no reopening date. The Oakland Bay Bridge was shut down indefinitely. Through Chicago, I-90 closed. The states did not have the resources to fix the aging roads. The I-76 bridge over the Delaware river collapsed, killing 23 people and injuring 43 others. Governments across the country had no reason to believe the situation was going to get any better.

The Dow Jones Industrial Average dropped 2,000-points in 2042, finishing at 11,231. The GDP continued to decrease, dropping 21 percent on weak economic activity.

Total revenue to the US government was only $1.75 trillion. The federal debt at the end of 2042 was $188 trillion. With a budget to ensure another $16.9 trillion scheduled for 2043, the total debt at the end of 2043 was $207 trillion.

2043

I WAS SWORN into the Senate for a second term. I moved up in seniority in my committees, and because of the strong showing by Republicans in the mid-term elections, I began an exploratory committee to run for president. With a popular incumbent president and his hand-picked successor (the new vice president), few other Republicans were willing to run. Historically American voters had chosen sweet-tasting poison over sour medicine. However, I believed this administration was vulnerable to an upset with the economy in freefall and crime climbing.

My exploratory committee was upbeat and believed I could defeat the vice president. I approached Republican leadership to garner their support. They openly admitted they had doubts about a junior senator from Texas holding his ground against such a seasoned politician like the vice president, but they had few other options. Plus, they had seen my work in committees and on the bipartisan committee the president appointed me to serve. I had handled myself well. I won the support of the minority leaders in the Senate and House of Representatives. I quietly formed the key components of my campaign committee and began increasing my national profile. The Republican National Committee had to remain neutral until there was an official candidate, but they had resources available to all Republican hopefuls that I could access.

My national exposure crusade started slow, but I began receiving more inquiries as I performed well on different media networks. It did not take long before one of the anchormen asked if I was running for president. The time was not ideal for me to announce. I believed my organization was ready to launch, but this was not the forum. I sidestepped the question. I had my campaign team put together a media blitz. Two weeks later, with my family at my side, I had a news conference and announced my candidacy for the presidency of the United States of America.

My campaign targeted the economy and excessive spending by the federal government. These were the issues that burdened Americans. I had to place the blame squarely on the sitting president's shoulders and hope that it tainted the vice president. I was not foolish enough to believe the Republicans were not partially culpable but admitting that was not how you win elections.

I promised to lower spending and redirect our country to the prosperity we once knew. We would enforce immigration law, stop reducing military spending, and return law and order to our streets.

I was neglecting my senatorial duties, but my staff kept me apprised of legislation on the floor that would benefit from my involvement. Although the Democrats still controlled both Houses, Republicans continued to push legislation. After the last election, more Democrats were receptive to crossing the aisle and supporting legislation that would help them keep their seats, even if it meant working with the opposition.

Once I announced my candidacy, the media coverage became intense, and they hounded my family everywhere. My friends and colleagues had a barrage of questions, e-mails, and text messages thrown at them. No part of my life was unexamined.

* * *

THE PRESIDENT WAS blaming the high interest rates on everybody and everything but himself, but at 82 percent inflation, it was hard to shield himself from much of the responsibility. The attacks kept coming and were beginning to make a dent in his vice president's electoral lead. He countered with the few federal benefits that remained for the poor and took credit for reducing a costly military. He was working hard to get his vice president elected.

To save money without costing votes, the president notified the United Nations that the United States would be withdrawing its financial support. That would include the building and security. If the organization wanted to continue occupying the New York facility, they would need to pay a market-based rent and fund their own security. As an alternative, the UN could purchase the building—but they would be taxed.

One academic study found most farm subsidies were going to corporate farms. Those corporations were making 20 percent profits because of the subsidies. Based on that one study, Congress eliminated 95 percent of farm subsidies and made it illegal for a corporation to receive any benefits. This was not popular with the family farmers, who found it much harder to qualify for the payments. Many single-family farmers had filed as a corporation for previous tax benefits; now, they were losing their tax break and being denied subsidies. This drove some families out of the farming business and caused the rest to raise their prices, further aggravating inflation.

All levels of government were feeling the pain of lost revenue, increased demand for services, and stifling inflation. Municipalities were seeking aid from the federal government to help fund police, fire, and hospitals. Unfortunately, the federal government was unable or unwilling to help. They had their own problems on a much bigger scale. As cities grappled with funding basic services, streetlights went unrepaired and stoplights failed. The sewer systems backed up, and trash piled up around the cities. The electrical system was decaying; the rolling blackouts becoming permanent for larger parts of the country. There was increasing unrest in the streets.

There was an airplane crash in Chicago. A Boeing 787 carrying 296 passengers and 12 crew members went down. The investigation claimed it was a mechanical failure due to poor maintenance procedures. The media claimed the Federal Aviation Administration (FAA) failed to provide adequate oversight due to budget cuts and poor leadership. The FAA denied those accusations. The fact was the FAA had large budget cuts in recent years, and their manpower was at 60 percent. They were having difficulty finding capable applicants, and many believed the administration was hiring unqualified technicians.

As markets fell, companies cast off jobs, and unemployment became an even bigger problem. Suicides quadrupled in three years. The Dow Jones Industrial Average dropped 3,500-points to 7,940, and the national GDP decreased by 43 percent. Tax revenue dropped below $1.4 trillion.

The federal debt at the end of 2042 was $207 trillion. With a budget to ensure another $17 trillion scheduled for 2043, our continued total debt at the end of 2043 was $227 trillion without considering any natural disasters or unexpected military charges.

2044

IN THE FIRST eight months, I continued to build on my popularity with no significant scandals to set me back. By the Republican Presidential Convention in August, I won the nomination easily. Delegates liked my acceptance speech and jump-started my campaign on a positive note. However, the sitting vice president was still leading in the polls by a large margin.

Although I wanted to keep it a clean and civil campaign, that didn't last long. After the vice president claimed my political career benefited from exploiting the poor in favor of my corporate cronies and disparaged my close ties to China, I began to fight back. I demonstrated that the vice president, in his long career in politics, practiced poor financial management and egregious partisan bickering rather than doing what was best for the people he represented. I took every opportunity to stress the dire straits the country was in and placed the blame squarely on the agenda of the liberal policies of the Democratic party.

I stressed the need for a smaller government that was less intrusive in the lives of Americans. I promised to reduce regulations on businesses so they could thrive, allowing them to start hiring more people and put America back to work. I would reduce taxes where I could, but with the current deficits, most of those would have to wait until the country was on a surer financial footing. I would encourage businesses to help address homelessness in their cities.

Our military was a shell of its former glory. I wanted to rebuild our national defense, so we could help the world be more peaceful. Our first priority must be to keep our country safe. The military was the key to that process, but it was not the only thing. Our borders had to be secured. We needed migration from all parts of the world. We needed to pull the best and brightest to help rebuild our workforce. Once we regained our strength, we could refocus our attention on the less fortunate people in the world.

Our roads and cities desperately needed rebuilding. We could not continue to build and not understand that we needed to maintain those resources. We must run our finances in a responsible way. When a road needed repair, resources would be available to repair or replace that thoroughfare. The same was true for airports, train stations, and railroad tracks. These are the things government had to do to ensure businesses had less friction in getting their goods to market.

* * *

AGAIN, INVESTORS DEMANDED more interest to entice them to buy our treasury bonds. The Federal Reserve raised the rate by 0.5 percent. The bonds sold, but they moved slowly.

California was unable to make its bonds' payments and defaulted. Historically, bondholders would lose much of their equity, but because investors saw them as low-risk investments, the chance was worth taking. Because of the poor showing of municipal bonds through the past 20 years, investors required more protection than before. These defaulted California bonds were the first municipal bonds that allowed investors to receive partial ownership of the resource that the bond was issued to fund. This gave the investors a minority claim on the major California airports and seaports.

Although this was a devastating event for California, they were not alone in their suffering. Most major cities were declaring martial law and curtailing many of their citizen's civil rights. Curfews were a norm. Gatherings of more than 15 people were prohibited. Concealed carry weapons permits were a thing of the past. Unfortunately, enforcement was difficult because laws were in place restricting police enforcement. Even if the police did act, there were not enough jail cells to store the accused. The National Guard was also ineffective. After years of military spending cuts, morale was low, equipment was in disrepair, and after the failed coup d'état, leadership was not receptive to supporting law enforcement.

All remaining foreign subsidies stopped. The president was surprised how quickly countries that had previously been our allies turned on us. For over a hundred years, the US had sent money, food, medicine, and troops to help these countries, costing America trillions of dollars. Now that we were in need, they abandoned us. It seemed that in international politics, loyalty was just a talking point. The only thing that mattered was what we were doing for them now.

The reduced GDP caused massive shortages in necessities. There were lines in supermarkets, but little food available for the few who could afford to pay. Gas lines reminiscent of the 1970s formed across the country, and considering few had the funds to buy gas, these lines were enormous. Every charity organization had much more demand than resources to fill the needs. America was hurting.

The suffering did not end with financial heartache. There was an earthquake in the Pacific Ocean that caused a tsunami to hit San Francisco. The damage and loss of life were massive. The federal government was unable to provide much assistance. The result was an agonizingly slow recovery and many more lives lost.

November 8 was election day. Due to anomalies in mail-in ballots that had persisted since 2020 and numerous recounts in 18 states and 247 counties, the final results were unknown until December 16. The US Supreme Court ruled the counting complete to allow the Electoral College to vote on December 19. Jesse Wright convinced the electorate that a Wright presidency would do a better job at fixing US problems. In a hotly contested election, Jesse Wright became the first Republican President of the United States since 2020. He won only 271 electoral votes—the minimum required to win.

The outgoing president was considering the ramifications of defaulting on bonds. His party's leadership convinced him the damage to our economy and our ability to borrow money in the future would be horrific. He allowed the problems of America to fall on the incoming president's shoulders.

Although the Dow Jones Industrial Average declined 1,700 points for the year, there was a modest uptick after the election. The president-elect took that as a good sign for his prospects. There was only $1.15 trillion in revenue for the year.

The federal debt at the end of 2043 was $227 trillion, with a budget to ensure another $21.8 trillion scheduled for 2044. The total debt at the end of 2044 was $250 trillion.

2045

AS PRESIDENT-ELECT, I spent January putting my cabinet in place. This was challenging because I did not have a group of former Republican cabinet members from which to choose. It had been 25 years since a Republican was a cabinet member. Because Democrats dominated Congress, if I selected legislators, there was a possibility the states would fill the position with more Democrats. Instead, I sought prominent company CEOs, but few were willing to leave their more lucrative jobs and face the prospect of an adversarial confirmation process. The result was a cabinet that was weak and ineffective.

January also showcased legal fights related to the election—if the Democrats were successful at changing the results in one state, it would change the election results. As with previous elections, the Supreme Court was reluctant to adjudicate the issues, preferring to let the states control their own elections—as dictated by the US Constitution. Most of the lower court's rulings were in my favor. The courts were reluctant to change the vote without significant evidence of wrongdoing.

On January 20, 2045, I became the 50th President of the United States. The inauguration had many in attendance. With 29 years since the last Republican inauguration, conservatives were excited to see a Republican take the Presidential Oath of Office. My inaugural address focused on our government's fiscal responsibility. The goal was to reduce unemployment and get people back to work. Getting inflation under control was also a heavy emphasis of the speech. These goals would be difficult to achieve since the US Congress and Senate remained in liberal Democrat control, and bipartisanship was not a trait of current politics in America.

* * *

AFTER TAKING OFFICE, President Wright received detailed briefings on all facets of the scope of office. First was a damning explanation of the current status of the nation's debt, high interest rates on US bonds, and recent problems funding the increasing deficits. Advisors discussed options for reducing the deficits, minimizing debt interest payments, and how to get the economy out of the depression. The president began to feel the weight of the office immediately.

The president's next briefing was by the Joint Chiefs of Staff on military readiness. Military strength was almost nonexistent, with many of our troops brought home from overseas. This weakened our relationship with many allies that had become dependent on our military and financial support. Our adversaries gained strength while US abilities diminished.

Civil unrest across America was increasing as citizens protested the lack of jobs, inflation, and availability of necessities. All major cities had protests that required additional resources that were not available. Thus, the damages of these protests were considerable. The infrastructure damage from the demonstrations piled on top of the neglected public works as the economy degraded. Inner city hospitals closed for the safety of their employees. Schools were closed as risks increased. Government employees were still getting paid as tax revenue plummeted. Municipal and state governments increased their demand for federal assistance. All of these issues exacerbated the financial plight of all levels of government.

President Wright weighed the limited options. First, the president needed to cut the size of the government. These austerity measures had consequences. Reducing the size of the government meant reducing employees, which would increase unemployment. A smaller government also meant fewer services to the most vulnerable citizens. These efforts would also inspire increased rioting resulting in additional damage as there were fewer resources to dampen the unrest. Next, the debt would be more costly as interest rates rose. All tax revenue currently paid the interest on the accumulated debt, meaning all governmental activity led to additional debt. Defaulting on the debt would be catastrophic. The current budget required additional borrowing, even if the debt went away. By defaulting, the interest on new bonds would be even higher than current requirements.

Finally, the military consumed over one-third of the federal government's budget. President Wright targeted the remainder of smaller bases for closure and personnel reductions at others. By cutting their funding, the president weakened an already demoralized organization. At the same time, cutbacks of people in uniform would worsen unemployment. With all the brilliant minds at the head of the US government, they could not find a tenable solution.

As the president continued reducing the size of the government, he proposed eliminating three cabinet-level positions and their departments. Four other departments received cuts of 40 percent, and all the others faced reductions of at least 20 percent. These cuts were not well received. Congress fought hard to minimize the reductions. Even if Congress accepted the president's cuts, it would have a marginal effect on total spending as most costs were for entitlements. So, the reductions Congress finally passed did little to address the problem.

The president also proposed the suspension of many payments to the states. State budgets relied on the federal government for 20.7 percent (Hawaii) to 46.1 percent (Montana) of their funding. Congress modified the reduction that varied based on the seniority of the legislator, again reducing the effectiveness of the president's initiative.

Next, President Wright directed his attention to reducing the debt by working with the organizations and countries that held US securities. China held 70 percent of the US's outstanding bonds. The president directed the chief of staff to coordinate a state visit and dinner with the People's Republic of China president.

The press did not treat the president or his initiatives well. The service reductions continued the red ink, and negative press coverage caused an increase in the already disruptive rioting across the country. These riots continued to cause infrastructure damage to roads, buildings, and utilities. Municipalities and the federal government did not have the resources for effective enforcement, further empowering the rioter to be more belligerent.

President Wright and his staff spent weeks preparing for the meeting with the president of China. Trade relations had worsened as the US financial situation became more tenuous. Finding the best way to broach reducing bond payments would be delicate. The administration decided to try to stress the benefits to China of lowering payments instead of the possibility of default.

Because of the across-the-board budget cuts, Congress started researching impeachment. The president's reduction in retired military benefits and lower social security payments caused a furor amongst recipients and legislators. Many representatives believed the reductions broke promises and were illegal because they failed to go through the legislative process. With a substantial Democrat majority, the Speaker of the House easily had the votes to impeach. There was less assurance in the Senate. Although Democrats had the majority, they could not convince 68 Senators to remove the president from office so soon after inauguration.

After months of negotiation, the president of China agreed to a state meeting in Washington, DC. The State Department was hesitant to be open about the president's planned agenda. Those issues would come to light when addressing the itinerary.

The president of the People's Republic of China was to arrive in Washington, DC, on December 4, 2045, with the state dinner planned for three days later. Once the Chinese president's airplane took off for the 13.5-hour flight, the White House received a message that the president was not aboard; he sent the foreign minister. The foreign minister was also a member of the Central Committee of the Communist Party of China, one of the highest cabinet positions—but he was not the president.

The Chinese said the foreign minister was the better person for the negotiations. His English was very good, which would prevent the negotiations from being polluted by translators. The minister also had experience with national financial issues and was highly trusted by the Chinese president. The US delegation believed the change was a negative development and gave the Chinese a tactical advantage. The clock was ticking on re-evaluating US negotiation tactics.

The foreign minister had 36 hours of rest to get over his jetlag. The negotiations started on December 6, 2045. The US State Department used the day to brief the Chinese foreign minister on the American financial situation. The secretary of state laid out a couple of options where the Chinese government could help relieve the economic pressures in the United States. The Chinese foreign minister listened intently without comment. As the briefings concluded, the foreign minister said he would consult with Beijing and continue negotiations the next day. He requested the US president, the chairman of the Joint Chiefs of Staff, and the chairman of the Federal Reserve to join the negotiations.

Tension was high as the dignitaries gathered to begin negotiations the next morning. When the meeting started, the foreign minister asked the Federal Reserve Chairman what the current total debt of the US federal government was. It was just over $250 trillion. The foreign minister said China's portion was $175 trillion. The Chinese government had begun questioning whether the US would repay its debt when it passed $100 trillion.

Directing his question to the president, the minister asked how the United States intended to repay their debt. The president reiterated the secretary of state's briefing from the day before and said the first step was to restructure the debt. He hoped China would be willing to forgive some of the debt and then reduce the interest payments of the remainder. Then, the US would work with other nations to do the same. In conjunction with revenue enhancements by increasing broad-based taxes and reducing subsidy payments to states, the country would get on a firmer financial footing. The US would also evaluate aid to foreign countries and international organizations like the United Nations, NATO, etc. The US would reduce the size of the government. A combination of these measures should put the US on the road to financial recovery.

The foreign minister listened to the president without comment. When President Wright finished, the foreign minister said he had several follow-up questions. He asked, "First, why now? Your country has been running ever-increasing deficits for 50 years. Why didn't your leadership correct this before now?"

President Wright did not have an answer.

The minister continued. "The US is at the point where all of its tax revenue is needed to service the debt. You have to borrow money for all of your federal government services. You passed the point where you could grow out of your debt 40 years ago. At that same time, China pulled hundreds of millions of people out of poverty. So, it is not a worldwide economic issue; it is an American problem. Why would we believe the US would change its ways if China gave you relief?

"During this same era, the US government has courted China's investments in America. They were encouraging China to purchase US debt. All the while claiming moral superiority over China and our government, placing tariffs on our products that America needed. You accused our country of manipulating our currency, stealing technology, and human rights violations. You used that power to bully other world leaders as well. You welcomed Chinese money but condemned us publicly.

"While the US was living beyond its means, China was building. Our currency is now the de facto world currency while the US dollar has diminished in prestige. This caused an influx of dollars into the market as countries divested themselves of US currency. This significantly increased inflation. While you were defunding your military, China was building. Now your military is weakened, and your nuclear defense is in disrepair. The recently attempted coup d'état further weakened your military capability. World governments are more willing to work with China because of their fear of your inability to repay debt and honor your commitments. This causes an increase in bond interest, further exacerbating your financial plight.

The result is the balance of power has changed. China is the dominant superpower, and the US is a distant second. Soon Russia may surpass your influence.

"Now you ask China to forgive a large portion of your debt and reduce interest payments on the remainder. Over the last thirty years, your government has manipulated its currency. You have maintained artificially low interest rates considering the amount of debt you've issued and the revenue your country collects. Thus, the US is already paying a sub-market rate on its bonds. Did the United States government believe we were investing in America for your benefit?"

The foreign minister asked the president, "How does China benefit from allowing the US to take these steps?"

President Wright was visibly disturbed by the Chinese foreign minister's assertions. He regained his composure and said, "The US would be forced to default on the bonds without substantial relief. In that case, China would lose its $175 trillion investment in the United States. This would mean you failed to renegotiate the bonds, which is the reason for your visit."

The foreign minister looked at the president and said, "Sir, my visit was not to renegotiate our bonds. It was to inform you that China will no longer be funding your debt. We have a vested interest in you not defaulting, and therefore cannot allow it. I would hope what is left of your intelligence community has informed you of significant Chinese naval activity. We have ten aircraft carrier battle groups off the coasts of the United States. Today is not a day of reconciliation; it is a day of reckoning.

"You and your citizens have stood on the shoulders of great men before you. Your schools have not educated, your people choose not to learn, and your politicians choose not to lead. You choose failure. Your citizens took everything and made little until there was nothing left.

"Countries fail from internal and external threats. Because of the minimal austerity steps that you have taken over the last couple of years, the riots in your major cities have intensified. With China pulling its future financial support, these disruptions will intensify. That would cause the riots to increase and eventually prevail. If that happens, your government will fall, and China will lose its investment. Not only will it lose its investment in your national debt, but also in the funding of your state, municipal, and special district projects. China cannot allow your internal threat to succeed. The other way governments fail is through external threats. China is your most pressing external threat today and has been for the past 40 years.

"Today, we give you an opportunity to save many lives. I am here to take control of the United States of America and make it a territory of the People's Republic of China. I and all of China want to make this transition without bloodshed. Your nation has boasted of a peaceful transition of power for nearly 300 years. We wish to continue that tradition. However, we are in a position to use force if required. We hold no animosity toward the American people. China has 20 cargo ships loaded with food, clothing, medicine, and other necessities ready to arrive over the next two weeks after China has control.

"Mr. President, I need an answer."

President Wright asked for time to consult with congressional leaders, White House lawyers, the Chief Justice of the Supreme Court, the Chairman of the Joint Chiefs of Staff, and the Federal Reserve.

The foreign minister said he had until the end of the day. He looked at the Joint Chiefs of Staff chairman and said, "The US military must stand down now. No airplanes are to take off. All those that are airborne will land at the nearest airport. No ship shall set sail. Those deployed will immediately return to the US. There will be no army troop movements. If these instructions are not heeded, the Chinese air groups will start attacking strategic infrastructure targets. If this situation comes to war, be warned the battles will be on US soil."

In the president's private study, the staff began coordinating with congressional leaders and the Chief Justice. The Chief Justice said there was no provision in the Constitution to relinquish the country's control to another sovereign power. The chairman of the Federal Reserve confirmed the dire financial situation.

The Joint Chiefs of Staff chairman said, "Military readiness is poor, with less than 20 percent of army units' mission-ready, 17 percent of naval resources mission ready, and 23 percent of air force resources available. Our stockpile of ammunition and fuel has been depleted with funding cuts." The chairman did not believe the country's nuclear arsenal was reliable and feared the Chinese missiles were superior. The chairman further claimed that a conflict with China on US soil would result in millions of American causalities.

The Speaker of the House of Representatives and the majority leader in the Senate were dumbstruck by the predicament and had difficulty accepting the situation before them. After heated discussions, they all reluctantly agreed that the US was in no position to challenge the Chinese.

The president returned to the oval office and informed the Chinese foreign minister that the

United States of America was now subservient to the People's Republic of China.

The foreign minister said he would brief the press from the Truman Balcony at 6:00 PM on December 7, 2045. He directed the president to have the US flag removed from the White House. Further, the president and vice president were told the country no longer needed their services and to retire to their residences with their families.

At 6:00 PM, the Chinese foreign minister walked out on the Truman Balcony to a confused press corps. The Chief Justice of the Supreme Court, the Chairman of the Joint Chiefs of Staff, the Chairman of the Federal Reserve, and the foreign minister's aide joined him. He was very direct and stated, "The United States of America was now a territory of the People's Republic of China," to stunned silence. He continued and announced the president and both houses of Congress had been relieved of their authority. The laws of the People's Republic of China now governed this land. Within days, humanitarian aid would begin arriving at American ports carrying food, medicine, clothing, and other essentials. The Chinese government and its people held no animosity toward the people of this country.

He said, "Your government failed you, and China will repair your ills. Over the last 50 years, we have lifted hundreds of millions of people out of poverty. We will do the same here. From this day forward, the United States of America is no more."

With those words, the Chinese flag rose over the White House. The foreign minister concluded with, "We now stand in the PEOPLE'S REPUBLIC OF AMERICA."

THE END

George Washington supposedly believed the most important personal value was courage, and the most important institutional value was fiscal responsibility.

* * *

"Your children's children will live under communism. You Americans are so gullible. No, you won't accept Communism outright, but we'll keep feeding you small doses of Socialism until you will finally wake up and find that you already have Communism. We won't have to fight you; We'll so weaken your economy until you fall like overripe fruit into our hands."
- Nikita Khrushchev

* * *

Ben Franklin was asked, "Doctor, what have we got? A republic or a monarchy?" To which Franklin supposedly responded: "A republic, if you can keep it."

* * *

"Tyranny naturally arises out of democracy."
- Plato